On the loveliest day of all, Arthur declared his love.

"I planned to wait," he huskily said. "Now we don't know what is ahead. Inga, one day when all this is over and I have completed my atonement, will you be my wife?"

Color stained her fair face, as fresh as the Indian paintbrush blossoming at the foot of the great rock where they sat. She stared at him, then opened her lips to reply.

Arthur forestalled her. "Before you answer, consider well." He turned from her clear, blue eyes to the smiling land around them. "I don't know where God may call me to serve. It may not always be on the *Flower of Alaska,* or even near the sea you love, that is so much a part of you. I want you to be happy, daughter of a hero."

She turned her face toward the west. Arthur followed her gaze. Beyond the mountains, past the broad, swampy river valleys, the low rolling hills, the mighty ocean roared. Somewhere hundreds of miles west and south, Lars Nansen faced wind and wave, waiting for his beloved daughter to rejoin him.

COLLEEN L. REECE is one of the most popular authors of inspirational romance. With over ninty books in print, including sixteen **Heartsong Presents** titles, Colleen's army of fans continues to grow. She loves to travel and at the same time do research for her historical romances. Colleen resides in Washington state.

Books by Colleen L. Reece

Don't miss out on any of our super romances. Write to us at the following address for information on our newest releases and club information.

Heartsong Presents Readers' Service
P.O. Box 719
Uhrichsville, OH 44683

Flower of Alaska

Colleen L. Reece

The Flower Chronicles

Heartsong Presents

A note from the Author:
I love to hear from my readers! You may correspond with me by writing:

Colleen L. Reece
Author Relations
P.O. Box 719
Uhrichsville, OH 44683

ISBN 1-55748-918-1

FLOWER OF ALASKA

Cover illustration by Kathy Arbuckle.

prologue

Rising wind molded Inga Nansen's garments to her rigidly held body. It flirted with the sunny plaits wrapped around her shapely head and restored sparkle to eyes blue as a Norwegian fjord in the land of her mother's people. "Hero's daughter," by name and upbringing, Inga stood on the Seattle shore, one hand raised, heart breaking but too proud to weep. She had known since childhood her dreaded someday must come. Now she raised her head higher, spurning both regret and cowardice as unworthy of her heritage. "I can endure," she told the lashing waves. "Each moment brings me closer to my next someday." A smile curved her lips skyward and added beauty to her face. "Until then, I shall make Father proud."

From the deck of the *Flower of Alaska*, Captain Lars saw his daughter through a mist delicate as dawn over a tranquil sea. So had his beloved wife Astrid once stood, like a figurehead on an ancient Viking ship. His face twisted with pain. Impossible to believe eighteen long years had passed since the fateful day he sailed into Boston harbor after being delayed by unspeakable storms, only to find his wife not waiting for him at the harbor.

A twinge of disappointment had surged through his sturdy, Swedish body. Although Astrid had no way of knowing when he would arrive, a secret desire to see her standing in the exact spot from which she had waved farewell months earlier lay deep in his heart. Always before she had been at his

5

side, exulting in the wildest gales, clinging to his arm with salt spray drenching her blonde hair, laughing while the ship pitched and tossed and Lars prayed to God for deliverance.

The day he sailed alone Astrid's eyes had been deep, mysterious pools. "I will remain behind," she told him. When he opened his mouth to protest, she laid strong fingers over it. "You will not be gone long. When you return, I will have a surprise for you."

How could he demur when she held up soft lips to be kissed? He gathered her against his heart, knowing the memory would warm him on his journey. But Lars had returned to discover the woman he loved more than life itself and second only to the God of sky and sea had slipped away. She left behind a tiny scrap of helpless humanity. The stricken captain looked into a miniature Astrid's face, complete with the pink and white complexion he knew and loved. If only he had not gone! Why hadn't she told him of the miracle to come into their lives? Yet they had not planned on his being gone so long. Had he not been held up by every adversity known to mankind, he would have been with Astrid in her time of greatest need.

Lars Nansen came from a line of men who refused to whine even when life dealt its harshest blows. He permitted a sister to raise Inga only until he felt capable of caring for her in his sea-roving life. The day she turned five, she became her father's "Honorary First Mate," defying, as had her mother, the superstition that women brought bad luck to sailing vessels.

The flaxen-haired child took to the sea with all the fervor of her Scandinavian background. Season followed season and melted into years as glaciers thawed in the spring. By the early 1890s, the Nansens had abandoned the East Coast for the more challenging West. First California lured them and then Washington Territory that had recently become a state. Inga thrived. Seldom did sickness lay its dreaded finger on her. Yet from the day she first stepped foot on her father's clipper ship, the *Norseman,* always the time of reckoning loomed ahead, strange and unwelcome to her satisfied soul.

After she grew old enough to read the Roman orator Cicero's writings, she exclaimed, "It's like the fabled Sword of Damocles, suspended by a single hair above me and ready to fall." She wrinkled her nose.

"With one difference," Lars teased. "The sword never fell but when you are eighteen, you will go to college. With the help of God and good books, I can teach you much. You must, however, learn to make your own way should the sea claim me."

"As if it could," she scoffed. Eyes brilliant, she leaned against him. "You are the best sailor on all of the seven seas." Still, her body quivered.

He abruptly changed the subject. "I hanker to try something new. Inga, what would you say if we sell the *Norseman*?"

She looked astonished. "You don't mean to leave the sea!"

He shook his shaggy blond head. "I wish to purchase one of the newer ships, a vessel powered by steam. Think of it. We would no longer be dependent on the capricious winds. I also have a hankering to see Alaska Territory." His blue eyes glowed. "Think, a new land, unspoiled, nay, nearly untouched."

Her enthusiasm matched his, yet caution overrode desire. They methodically studied everything they could find concerning steamships. They spent hours discussing both charted and uncharted waters off the rugged Washington and western Canadian coast, the Inside Passage between Canada and

Vancouver Island. Most often, their gaze rested on maps of the far-off mysterious Alaskan coastline that beckoned them with all the lure of the mythical sea sirens.

They considered countless ships. None suited both until they fell in love with the *Flower of Alaska*, up for sale in Seattle following the death of its owner. "Who can resist such a durable ship, especially with such an enticing name?" Inga demanded. Her eyes glistened with pride and anticipation when her father signed the papers. He insisted they be made out as jointly owned by Lars and Inga Nansen, with full ownership automatically reverting to the other in the event of death of either owner.

"Your dowry," he told her. "She'll take us anywhere we choose to go." Lars affectionately patted the newly painted white hull. A smile made deep creases around his weather-wise eyes. "Inga, what do you think of sacrificing some of the cargo space to make a few rude staterooms for passengers? Nothing fancy, mind you, just a clean place for sleeping. If we let it be known we can carry a few persons interested in seeing Alaska Territory, we might pick up passages now and then."

She readily agreed but secretly rejoiced no one signed on for the first *Flower of Alaska* voyage. Somewhere in the Pacific Ocean, she would celebrate her eighteenth birthday. The next sailing meant separation from father, companion, best friend. The knowledge enhanced the trip. Inga's hungry gaze memorized every timbered inlet, each shining glacier, every flaming dawn and purple dusk. Nothing escaped her farseeing eyes. Grazing deer and moose, bears batting salmon to their cubs, slinking coyotes and wolves that stared at the *Flower of Alaska* and made her feel an intruder became memories to hoard and draw from. The sight of a soaring eagle brought unshed tears. Jutting white peaks frowned down on them and filled her with awe. Always Inga had known God and the Son who came to save those who accepted Him, but nothing in her travels proclaimed His handiwork with the sheer sublimity of the Last Frontier.

"Someday I want to go inland," she told Lars. "I want to run beside a dogsled until I am tired, then wrap myself in furs and ride until I am able to run again. Oh, this glorious land!"

For a single moment Lars's determination wavered. *Father,* he silently prayed. *Am I wrong in forcing this unspoiled, innocent child of Yours to forsake the life she loves? What can even the learned men at the university do for her that I have not? How will she face a new world, one she fears?* An instant later Lars set his jaw in a hard line. They had thrashed it out a hundred times before enrolling her at the University of Washington, now thriving after its modest beginning in 1861.

"It is not just that you need more education than your father possesses," Lars admitted. "Inga, we are so close you have made no friends other than those who sail with us. It is time you see past the horizon our love for one another has set. God in His mercy may well grant us many more happy years together. Still, you need others in your life, girls and young men—"

She cocked her head to one side and laughed merrily. "So at last you tell me what is in your Swedish head." She placed her hands on her hips, elbows akimbo. "I think you fear you shall have no grandchildren if you do not send me to school so I shall not be a *dummkopf.*"

"As if you could ever be that," he scoffed.

The girl's laughter faded. "Do you think any man worthy

to be your son will care whether I know all the university teaches? Did Mother say before accepting you, 'Lars, I must see the paper that tells me you are wise enough to be my husband?'" Her laugh rang out again. "The only papers she cared about were those that showed you capable of setting your course by the North Star and holding steady in time of storm." Moisture glinted on her lashes and her smile grew tremulous. "If God wishes me to become a wife, He will provide me with a mate, will He not?"

It had taken all Lars's strength to keep insisting in the face of such trust. Now something deep inside whispered a few words that set his head spinning. All along, Inga had known the plans and rebelled as much as possible without actually refusing to attend the university. Suppose he put it straight to her. If she were to make the final choice, would she not be far more satisfied, or at least resigned to the years ahead?

The daring idea took root and grew. That evening when the *Flower of Alaska* lay anchored in a calm, old-rose sea highlighted with saffron, Lars rested his arms on the ship's rail next to those of his daughter. The afterglow painted her in shades of pink, adding an ethereal loveliness offset by the simple gray gown she had donned for the evening meal.

"Inga, you know my reasons for sending you to college and why. You have just passed your eighteenth birthday and are more young woman than girl. I have watched you steer this ship as well as I ever could do. First Mate, if you still want to stay with me, so be it."

Disbelief gave way to radiance. A rush of hastily swiped tears gleamed on her face in silver streaks. "Father, do you really mean it?"

"I do." To his surprise, she didn't answer immediately. Instead, she looked out over the glowing water, into the darkening sky, everywhere except at him.

Once Lars had hooked an enormous fish. It writhed and struggled, putting up such a grand fight he could not bear it. To the disgust of his crew, he freed the magnificent creature. Inga's expressive face showed she, too, fought—one of the hardest battles of her life. Lars clamped his lips together to keep from telling her she need not choose but could simply keep on as they had. Nay. She had fought physical storms and won. She must fight this one, unaided by him.

"You know I want to stay." She looked at him with such appeal in his eyes he nearly weakened again.

"I know."

"Will you be disappointed?" A quaver ran through her musical voice, a minor note of fear and pain.

"I have faith you shall choose the way best for you, child." He cleared his throat and made a hasty retreat, unwilling to chance remaining with her. "You need not decide now," he called over one shoulder and glanced back.

Her face took on the mother-of-pearl tints reflected in sky and sea. "You are wrong, Father. If I do not choose at this moment, I shall not have the courage." She came to him, eyes lustrous in the rapidly fading light. "The next time you sail, I shall wave farewell from the shore."

❧

The *Flower of Alaska* steamed farther out into Puget Sound. From his position at the helm, Lars Nansen watched Inga shrink to doll size. He had asked her not to watch the ship out of sight, and he saw her turn to face the city of Seattle and her new life.

Lars' keen gaze riveted on the still figure. Only the set of his daughter's shoulders, rigid and square as a soldier standing at attention, kept him from going back.

one

A lifetime ago Arthur Baldwin had rejoiced because his name meant noble. A lifetime ago he devoured tales of the legendary King Arthur who sought to rule by right, not might. A white flame of passion burned in the lad and he read the stories until he could quote long passages flawlessly. Like the king whose name he proudly carried, Arthur had been born to wealth and position, scion of an aristocratic Philadelphia family. Inspired by the days of chivalry, he had vowed to make of his inheritance a silver sword, dedicated to bringing peace and joy into a dark, sin-bound world—a lifetime ago.

One act of jealous rage had changed everything. His useless sword lay blackened by betrayal, its keen blade forever dulled. Not a trace remained of its former gleam, shining as the surgical instruments his long, tapered fingers used so skillfully.

Now Arthur sprawled in a costly chair in his Philadelphia red-brick mansion, staring into a fireplace with ashes dead as his dreams and ideals. His mussed blond hair with the deep wave no amount of brushing could remove, troubled eyes, and cherublike countenance masked a brilliant mind, but the cheerful, boylike features could not mask the load of guilt and remorse he carried.

Arthur turned his lackluster blue gaze toward the library door when it opened. The man he would be thirty years from now strode across the oriental rug.

"Why aren't you properly dressed for dinner?" Icicles clashed in the contemptuous voice, no colder than his blue eyes and frozen face. Arthur Baldwin, Senior's disapproving glance swept over his carelessly garbed son. "No gentleman is found in such attire at this hour." He gestured with the fine cigar adding its heavy scent to the already oppressive atmosphere.

"Is that all you have to say to me after what I did?" Arthur sprang to his feet, hoping for the tirade he richly deserved.

It didn't come. Not a muscle moved in his father's face. "All's fair. Haven't I taught you the important thing is winning?" He uttered an oath. "Don't tell me you're such a mollycoddle it makes you squeamish to use another's weakness to get what you want." He tossed the cigar into the fireplace. What passed for a smile spread over his face. "With Bern Clifton disqualified, you get the girl *and* the hospital appointment—"

"Bern's girl and position until I betrayed him," Arthur bitterly reminded. All the years of David-and-Jonathan friendship through college and medical school rose to accuse him: the friendly rivalry, the sharing of honors in classroom, operating theater, and on the athletic field. Competition brought out the best in the fair-haired Arthur and Bern, with his soot-black hair and eyes. Both stood at six feet, weighed in at 170. They worked together like blades of a fine pair of scissors, without malice, until the fateful spring evening when Arthur coaxed Bern from his studies to attend a party at Professor Langley's home.

A heavy hand descended on Arthur's shoulder. He turned his attention back to his frowning father, glad to temporarily shut out the last fourteen months.

"You did what anyone would do in like circumstances."

Protective numbness fled and brought him back to pulsing, unbearable life. "I did what none save a craven coward would even consider." Pain thickened the son's voice, and he flung off the authoritarian hand.

"You did what you had to do." Baldwin raised a supercilious eyebrow. "Agreed it is a nasty business but the hospital directors, Julia Langley, and all of Philadelphia have a right to know Clifton is nothing but a half-breed, as your private investigator discovered."

"He is also one of the two finest men I ever knew," Arthur said fiercely. Steel entered his spine. He took a menacing step toward the older man, fists clenched. "Never let me hear you call him that again."

For the first time in his life, the senior Baldwin fell back. He reached for another cigar, bit off and discarded the end, then lighted it deliberately. He exhaled a cloud of smoke that reminded Arthur of the detective's office where he had gone in an effort to unearth something that would discredit his rival. Would to God he had been struck dead on the street before he reached it.

His father's voice held a conciliatory note. "Don't take it so hard. Clifton's a talented surgeon. He'll have no trouble finding work—except in Philadelphia, of course."

"He's already learned that and gone," Arthur dully reported.

"Good. I understand the hospital wants you to start immediately. The directors said the sooner you begin the quicker this unfortunate incident will die down. Julia feels the same." His heavy brows came together. "In view of the late unpleasantness, she's willing to have a quick and quiet wedding, even to postpone the honeymoon for a time. In fact, your mother is at the Langleys' now making arrangements. I put a down payment on a fine piece of property not more than a mile from your new hospital. Julia wants a southern colonial-style home. Until it's built you can have the east wing here."

Arthur stared in disbelief. Rage equal to that which led to his downfall attacked him. "Unfortunate incident? Late unpleasantness? I destroy a man and you babble of position and land?"

"Can't you get it through your skull? Nothing stands between you and what you've always wanted: fame, power, wealth." Baldwin crushed his big fingers into a ball and squeezed. Angry red streaked his massive face.

Arthur straightened to full height and looked straight at his father. "Everything stands between. You can't honestly believe I will marry Julia and take a position won by foul means!"

Fear leaped to the watching eyes. "Why not? Clifton is out of the running."

All hope of establishing understanding between them fled. "'To the victor belongs the spoils,'" Arthur quoted. "Not this time. I wouldn't marry Julia if my life depended on it. The only thing I am thankful about in this whole mess is that Bern Clifton escaped a life of misery with a vain, vindictive woman."

His voice rang in the silence and his face twisted. "What hurts most is that *I always knew her for what she was.* Even when I told myself she might change if she married the right man, I knew better. Father, I betrayed the man who took the place of the brother I never had." Arthur's voice dropped to a whisper. "I sold my honor and my soul. Not for thirty pieces of silver. For a Jezebel not fit to wipe the feet of the Indian girl Benjamin Clifton married, who died giving birth to his son. I'd sooner bring a nest of vipers into my home than have anything further to do with Julia Langley." The deadly words fell into the thickening air like lead bullets.

Crack. Arthur staggered from the force of the open-handed blow across his left cheek. He had seldom been punished as a boy; never had his father struck him in the face. A mocking smile tilted Arthur's lips. "Strange how Philadelphia aristocracy upholds rank dishonor and abhors the truth."

The other's face turned apoplectic. "Silence! You will either accept the position that should have been yours from the first and marry a girl worthy of the house of Baldwin or you are no longer my son."

"Do you really mean that?" A thrill went through Arthur. His twisted reasoning whispered that such an act would be just punishment for what he had done.

"I do." His father folded his arms across his chest, face turned to granite.

"Very well. I will pack and leave immediately." Now that the ax of retribution had fallen, Arthur felt curiously light.

An unpleasant smile touched Baldwin's lips. He cocked his head to one side, measured Arthur's tall, strong frame, and played his trump card. "I will change my will tomorrow. Until the day you come to your senses and do what I say, you will receive not so much as a dollar."

Arthur looked at the proud old man and suddenly felt sorry for him. How must it feel to banish the son who had been his father's greatest hope? The thought gentled his voice. "I have what Grandmother left."

His father snorted. "A mere pittance. You'll never be able to live on such a paltry sum. Don't expect me to change my mind."

"I won't." He impulsively added, "I appreciate everything you have done for me. College, medical school, all this." He looked around the luxurious room.

"Enough to do what I ask?" A gleam of hope crept into the cold eyes.

Arthur could only shake his head. Why couldn't Father be more like Benjamin Clifton, whom Arthur loved? Agony went through him. In shaming Bern, he had also wounded his father. God grant that somehow, someday, he could redeem himself from the stain of sin indelibly etched on his hands. He laughed harshly. Benjamin Clifton's God would have no traffic with such as Arthur Baldwin.

"Where will you go?" his father demanded.

Words came of their own volition. "As far from Philadelphia as I can get."

Baldwin started for the door. He didn't look back, but hurled a final insult over his shoulder. "I never knew my only son would turn out to be a Judas to everything I stand for."

Arthur couldn't answer. All his life he had sought to earn his father's love. Much of his desire to best Bern had grown from longing to win the austere man's approval and bring triumph to one who considered first honors a Baldwin right. "I'll make you proud yet," he finally promised.

The bulky shoulders remained turned against him. The next moment, Arthur Baldwin, Senior, marched out of the library and out of his son's life without a word.

The young doctor waited until the footfalls crossed to the imposing dining room, and then he stepped from the library and dragged up the velvet-covered steps. He stumbled the length of the upper hall, entered his tasteful suite, and flung himself on the bed. His father's question beat into his brain. Where would he go? If Judas had not hanged himself, where would he have gone? Was there a place anywhere in the world where decent people would not shrink from him in horror if they knew what he was?

A light tapping at his door roused him from the half-stupor into which he had fallen. "Yes?"

A maid entered, bearing an envelope on a silver salver.

Arthur's heart leaped at sight of his name written in his father's bold, black scrawl. "Thank you." The door closed behind her. He ripped open the envelope and extracted a single heavy vellum sheet.

I will not have your mother troubled with all this, the missive read. *Should you change your mind, she need never know. I shall tell her you have gone away for a time. Thank God she is not home this evening. You will respect my wishes and not attempt to see her before you leave.* The message bore no signature.

"He thanks God." The laughter of irony bubbled in Arthur's throat and slipped out. What kind of God did Father worship, to condone treachery, then disclaim his son when he attempted to salvage a bit of honor? He tore the message to bits, wondering why it imposed no particular hardship. While he packed, Arthur thought of his childhood. Memories of this or that nurse tucking him in far outweighed the few times his diamond-decked mother rushed into the nursery to say goodnight before attending a party or ball. Relationship rather than love bound them. In a way, he had been as motherless as Bern Clifton. Arthur stopped folding clothing and stared at the damask draperies framing a spectacular afterglow. If he married Julia, his son—if she ever consented to have one—would see no more of his mother than he had as a child. Probably less. He shuddered and felt reprieved. The sun would come up in the west before that happened.

Arthur's first thought had been to leave Philadelphia that

night. He soon recognized the impossibility of his plan. Certain things required doing before he could shake the dust off his well-shined shoes. He frowned at the thought, finished his task, and ordered the family carriage brought to the front door. The well-trained driver failed to hide his curiosity but said nothing, even when he delivered his passenger to one of the more modest hotels. Warned by his father's jeering comment concerning available funds, Arthur had bypassed the more impressive lodgings. He slipped a bit of folded money into the driver's hand, smiled, and watched the carriage drive away.

Something stirred within him, feelings trying to be born. Outcast, unworthy of the companionship of his fellowmen, he yet possessed youth, strength, and medical skill. Long years stretched before him. Could hard work and service to others atone in some small measure for the sins he could not undo? The thought persisted and all through the long, sleepless night that followed, Arthur clung to it as a swimmer devoid of hope clings to a piece of wreckage.

≈

The following afternoon he walked into the august presence of the hospital directors with all the anticipation of a man facing the firing squad. His keen eyes looked around the hallowed circle. They would hire him, praise his skills. Some would even congratulate him on having the courage to expose Bern Clifton's parentage. Yet every man there secretly despised the brilliant young surgeon. It showed in their narrowed eyes and superior smirks.

The head man waved him to a chair. "Your father has given us to understand you will start in a few days," he rumbled. "Now, about salary—"

Arthur grasped at his remnants of manhood and prepared

to make his own short Declaration of Independence. He felt sweat crawl under his starched shirt. His hands turned clammy. For a craven moment, he hesitated. Was he a fool to throw away everything this revered band of men offered? To deliberately turn his back on his birthright? Both what he earned and would one day inherit could make a great deal of difference to those who needed help. Besides, what difference would it make to Bern, licking his wounds in some unknown place?

Even if he never knows, you will.

Arthur jerked. Had someone spoken? No, the directors awaited his reply. He squared his shoulders into the fighting stance that signaled his readiness to begin whatever hard task lay ahead. "My father has misinformed you. I thank you for considering me but I will not be taking the position." To his amazement, the words came clear and firm. A thrill of optimism shot through him.

"Do you want more money?"

Arthur wanted to laugh in the heavy-jowled face, whose owner was known to have grown wealthy by pandering to the rich and refusing to minister to those who could not pay. "No. I am leaving Philadelphia."

A gleam of avarice came to the sleek one's face. "Where are you going? I suppose a New York hospital has contacted you with a better proposition. Baldwin, we are prepared to meet, no, beat any offer you've received." He gave what passed as a laugh but sounded more like a gloat.

Arthur's lips twitched. He hadn't expected to find humor in this interview. "I prefer not to discuss my plans at this time." He disciplined a laugh. How these self-proclaimed paragons would jeer if he told them point-blank he had no idea where he was going once he walked from the room. He rose, a half-smile still on his lips. "Gentlemen, I bid you good day."

Arthur gracefully walked to the door and stepped through. Before it closed behind him he heard Dr. Smug growl, "A grandstand play to chisel more money out of us."

"He'll get it, too," a higher-pitched voice cut in. "He's the brightest star to come out of medical school in a decade, with the exception of Bern Clifton."

"We'll get him yet," the other promised. "Every man has his price. Let me talk with the Langley girl. She'll bring him around fast enough."

Arthur's eyes sparkled dangerously, boding no good for the plans being hatched behind the massive door. Should he go back in and let them have it with both barrels? He took one step. Stopped. What right had a Judas to call another man a sinner?

Somehow he got out of the hospital, fervently praying never to walk its sterile corridors again. Summer shimmered in the streets. A slight breeze cooled his hot face. Fragrance from a climbing rose wafted toward him. Conscious of his limited resources, Arthur made his way to the prestigious bank patronized by Baldwins for generations and made arrangements concerning his stipend from his grandmother's trust fund. Fortunately, he had not withdrawn the sum due him for the last quarter.

"I am leaving soon and am not sure where I will be. I will write instructions concerning payment of the next amount," he told the banker.

"Why—?" The man he had known since childhood broke off.

Arthur read shock in his eyes and knowledge that the heir to the house of Baldwin had not been expected to do anything so rash as to leave Philadelphia.

"Thank you. I'll be in touch." He pocketed bills, generous when it came to buying luxuries, but few on which to live.

All the way back to his hotel, Arthur fought a losing battle. If he were still a man, one thing remained to be done. Nay, two. The first proved easier than expected. He called at the Langleys, rejoiced to find Julia wasn't home, and left a note breaking all ties with her. Even if she refused to accept it, Professor Langley would recognize its blunt finality. Arthur felt ten pounds lighter when he left the house where he had whiled away many hours in flirtation. How blind he had been, how stupidly, arrogantly sure he could tame the temptress!

He ground his teeth in humiliation and started away. The longest two miles he'd ever faced lay between the Langley place and the modest Clifton cottage, more home than the red-brick mansion had ever been.

His courage dwindled with every inch. How could he face the father who once loved him as a second son? His coming might worsen things. If only he knew what had occurred the day Bern confronted his father. Arthur's steps slowed and faltered, but at last brought him to his destination. A light shone in the window, as it always did when dusk hovered. If only it were shining for him as in former days. His throat constricted. Despite his age, he longed to bound inside, throw himself at Benjamin Clifton's feet, and plead for mercy.

Arthur impulsively went forward. He stole around the house and peered into the open window from whence came the light—and a broken voice.

"Father, I have sinned in not telling Bern what he had the right to know. Forgive me. Be with him wherever he wanders. If Thou choosest not to bring him back to me, I beseech Thee, return him to Thy fold. And Arthur, who surely is tortured by what he has done. Help him to accept Thy forgiveness and learn to forgive himself. Into Thy hands I commend my boys. For Jesus' sake, amen."

Arthur could not intrude on such grief. Feeling more like Judas then ever, he stole away. Yet knowing the man he loved and respected above all others did not despise him lit a tiny candle of hope in his aching heart.

two

One year to the day after Dr. Arthur Baldwin left Philadelphia and his father's home, he climbed to the crest of the ridge above his rude cabin in western North Carolina and surveyed the valley below. His mobile lips turned up. He hadn't yet come to calling it "the Holler" as did those among whom he lived and worked. One day he would—if he stayed.

The valley that lay tucked in the folds of the Great Smoky Mountains like a cornhusk doll folded into a bit of leftover calico had become home to the outcast. Arthur sometimes felt he bore no relation to the Philadelphia doctor with all his affectations, who once poised on the pinnacle of success. Life in the mountains offered the contrast between civilization in all its self-imposed smugness and the challenge of survival on a daily basis. Engrossed in hacking out a new existence, "Doc Noble" as he was known, had gradually overcome the mountaineers' suspicion toward strangers and become one of them.

"Thanks to Donald," Arthur told a flock of crows bent on ravaging whatever cornfield they could attack. Their raucous caw-cawing had become so familiar he barely heard it. He flung himself on the needle-covered ridge and stared unseeingly at his cabin. Warmth flowed through Arthur. He closed his eyes, weary from being called out day and night by grave-faced men whose womenfolk had the miseries. Or babies who obstinately insisted on being born during the darkest night hours. Or those with summer complaint.

Hot sun baked the earth and put him into a state of torpor. Only the desire to evaluate the past months kept him from sleep. Arthur relived his aimless wanderings the first few weeks after he left Philadelphia. Despite the burden he carried, something deep inside thrilled to have broken free from the rigid future he'd mapped out early and religiously followed. His mouth twitched. For the first time in his life he had been free to wander. Yet his fingers had itched to hold his surgical instruments. His vow to redeem himself through service to mankind diminished the pleasure of answering to no one.

What quirk of Fate landed him in Asheville Arthur never knew. He remembered as if it were yesterday lingering long enough to wire his bank, then cashing his quarterly stipend. He thought how proud he had been to have survived with a few dollars left from his carefully hoarded store, supplemented by many piles of cut and stacked wood that paid for food and shelter. The palms of his hands bore calluses, yet he flexed his fingers continually. They must never be allowed to stiffen.

Why hadn't he realized how closely the shabby man with the moth-eaten moustache crowded behind him in line at the bank? Or that the sum he once considered paltry brought a gleam of greed to the watcher's pale eyes? Why had he cut through the alley on his way back to the rooming house? Arthur squirmed. If an inner awareness of something amiss hadn't caused him to whirl, he'd have been killed. He glimpsed his attacker and the murderous blow to his head glanced. He fell like a stone, making no outcry.

Arthur awakened in a strange room with white-washed walls, trying to piece things together in spite of his befuddled mind.

"Lie still, laddie," a voice with a soft Scottish burr ordered. "Ye were beset upon. I found ye, empty pockets and all. Ye will bide wi' me 'til ye are able to return to yer hoose, Dr. Noble."

A fresh wave of dizziness prevented Arthur from asking the thousand questions in his churning mind. A few hours later he awakened clear-headed, hungering and thirsting. His rescuer brought cold water, then Scotch broth, thick with vegetables and barley. He fed Arthur as though he had been a child, eyes kind in the seamed face beneath flossy silver hair.

"Who are you? How long have I been here? Why should you take me in?" Arthur asked when he could hold no more of the delicious broth.

Candid blue eyes smiled along with the Scotsman's lips. "I am Donal' MacDonal'. The sun has thrice risen and set since I found ye in sore need. Dr. Noble, dinna ye ken the Auld Book commands us to care for the stranger as if 'twere the Master Himself?"

"Why do you call me Dr. Noble?" Arthur shook his head and regretted it. A thousand little pain devils started hammering at his brain again.

"Laddie, ye talked some."

The quiet answer brought a scarlet tide to Arthur's face. He opened his mouth to correct his host, then slowly closed it. Only too well did he know how men babbled in delirium. He must have been remembering his childhood fascination with King Arthur and his pride in bearing the other's name. Why not let it stand? Traveling under a name so far removed from what he actually was could be a fitting part of his penance.

At Donald's suggestion, Arthur continued to "bide a wee"

in the older man's rented cottage. Donald went to his guest's
lodging place and returned with Arthur's possessions.
Excitement filled his eyes. "Ye are a docthor?"

"Yes."

"Praise to the Father!" Tears flowed. "Laddie, He has
brought ye to me."

Again Arthur bit his tongue. If he burst out with how un-
likely such a thing was, it would destroy the fragile tendrils
of friendship between them. He substituted, "Why would
you think that?"

"Ye canna ken how I've pleaded wi' God," Donald brokenly said. He went on to tell Arthur he had left his beloved
mountain home west of Asheville in the hopes of luring a
doctor to the remote area. So far he had failed miserably.
With autumn at its height and winter hovering in the forests, Donald knew he must go back soon. Just a few days
before he stumbled over Arthur in the alley he had confessed
his defeat to his Heavenly Father. "None weel gae," he said.
"Yet the mountain folk are God's childer, too. Must they die
wi'out the chance any docthor cud offer?" He paused and
spread both hands wide, eloquent in their appeal. "They
canna pay much but ye will nay go hungry. Weel ye coom?"

"Are you a minister?"

"Nay. I am only Donal' MacDonal' who loves the Lord
and His bairns, young and old."

A thrill went through Arthur. The God of Benjamin Clifton
and this worthy Scotsman's God must be the same. Had He
really and truly brought a modern-day Judas hundreds of
miles from his home in order to help a backwoods people?
"You believe God allowed me to be attacked and robbed so
your 'bairns' would have a doctor?"

"Nay, laddie!" Lightning flashed from the blue eyes. "Yet

since it happened, canna our Father bring good from it?"

His reasoning left Arthur speechless. A wellspring in his heart overflowed at the quick retort. He held out his hand but Donald waved it away, then placed both of his own on the young doctor's head. "Blest be ye."

The gentle touch of hands and benediction threatened the last of Arthur's composure. He hastily plied his new friend with questions, told a portion of his own past without going into details, and asked if he would be accepted in the "Hollow," which he'd learned meant valley.

"Aye. Ye weel be wi' me." Assurance rather than arrogance underlined every simple word.

A few days later, the mountain man and Philadelphia doctor began the strangest journey of Arthur's life thus far. Used to railway cars and fine carriages, he had to turn his head to keep amazement and bubbling laughter under control. Faced with a lop-eared mule named Lonesome whose chief virtue appeared to be laziness, Arthur discovered the most uncomfortable position in the world had to be astride that beast. Especially with him bent on plodding mile after irksome mile in the wake of Donald MacDonald, who calmly took for granted Arthur's younger years would overcome his inexperience.

At last they climbed the steeply sloping sides to the sharp summit of the ridge Donald called a hogback. Arthur experienced shock. Hazy mist gave the Great Smoky Mountains their name and extended as far as he could see. Highest and most rugged of the Appalachian system, Arthur could well believe they held the more than two hundred species of trees Donald had told him thickly forested the Smokies. To think such grandeur existed in his country and he had never known of it except through pictures that did little justice to the actual place! Like a blow came the knowledge: *This surely is not unique. Other parts of America must be equally majestic and inspiring. God willing, one day I will go and see.*

He roused from his reverie when Donald pointed below. "Laddie, we gae yon."

A lightning glance away from the mountains and into the hollow toppled Arthur's lofty ideas. Penniless for the next three months, dependent on the Scotsman for sponsorship, his future lay not in wild imaginings of travel to alluring places but in the Hollow. Autumn sun ruthlessly exposed both the picturesqueness and shortcomings of Arthur's new home. Patches of corn and other vegetables snuggled up to log cabins in cleared patches of the encroaching forests. Hounds bayed, their deep-throated cries clear in the still air. The laughter of children mingled high and sweet with the ring of pick and shovel on rock where men wrestled out stumps and cleared more land.

Arthur turned with a merry jest to his companion. Donald MacDonald's expression stilled him. If he lived to be a hundred he would never forget the poignant look in the blue eyes, the tone in the Scotsman's voice when he said, "Laddie, we're home." Silenced, the young doctor allowed Lonesome to pick his way down the winding, rutted trail into a new life.

≈

Arthur raised himself up with his elbows. Pine needles clung to his tousled blond hair. The same smoky haze that had lain over the mountains the day he came lingered, giving a bluish-gray cast to the forests. How he loved it! The view from the hogback above his cabin had offered refuge and strength when he felt he could not go on. Although Donald's simple introduction, "This is Dr. Noble," had given him a certain

status, the mountain folks' native distrust died hard. Arthur
felt himself on trial with every case. The presence of a "yarb
doctor," who probably killed as many as she cured with her
loathsome herbs and incantations, added further difficulties.
So did superstition and the ever-present resignation that hampered Arthur's work of healing.

In spite of—perhaps because of—opposition, "Doc Noble"
made inroads on disease and pestilence. The fierce competition he and Bern once good-naturedly waged served him in
good stead in the forgotten mountain hollow. Word ran from
cabin to cabin that "the fotched-on sawbones shore is a fighter.
Why, didn't he set up all night long with Miz Aken even
when the midwife said 'twas the Lord's will she be tuk? An'
ain't that young-un growin' stronger and bawlin' louder ever
minute since?"

Arthur laughed until he cried when Donald repeated it.
The older man's Scottish accent made it even funnier. Yet
the doctor's eyes shone with more than tears of amusement
when Donald added, "Ye done well, laddie."

"How can I even consider leaving?" Arthur whispered. "I
know I'm needed. I can give these people so much." He fell
silent, blue eyes shadowed. If he served the people of the
hollow all the days of his life he could never repay what
they had given him. Poor in things, caring little for much
save what was needed in their daily lives, they outstripped
Arthur's former acquaintances in generosity. He had seen
mothers whose children wore patched clothing
unhesitatingly give what they could ill afford when fire took
a neighbor's possessions. He had sat in service with them
both in the presence of a circuit-riding minister and when
Donald MacDonald read from his Auld Book. He had
marveled at prayers in the drawling dialect he'd grown to

recognize as peculiar to this part of the world.

Arthur thought of his associates in Philadelphia, always seeking, never satisfied. The mountain folk complained little and appreciated what they had. A new calico dress provided cause for rejoicing. So did a blushing teen girl and proud boy announcing they were promised; a good crop; abundant berries for jelly and preserves. If at times Arthur couldn't help comparing the simple play parties and singing school that offered fun in the midst of hardship with fancy balls back home he found not a twinge of regret. Stripped of the layers of veneer acquired by years of city living, Arthur found within himself the capacity for thankfulness over little things as great as in those he served.

"Laddie?"

Arthur looked up at the man he'd learned to love. Although the climb to the viewpoint rose steep and winding, Donald MacDonald breathed in his usual steady manner. He lowered himself to sit Indian fashion on the ground. Eyes bluer than the sky overhead looked straight at Arthur. "Ye weel be leaving us."

The young doctor didn't even ask how his friend knew. In the long months since they left Asheville, he'd come to appreciate the farsightedness of the Scotsman who rescued and cared for him. "Yes. No. I don't know."

"I dinna ken that answer." A trace of smile curled the thin lips.

"Part of me would be happy staying here forever," Arthur confessed. "It's a hard life but a good one." He swung his gaze back toward the mountain peaks. Between where they sat and the distant evergreens, the yellow-gold of autumn sparkled. Maple leaves whirled in their dance of death before plummeting to the earth's floor to await winter's burial shroud of white. "It's sad, isn't it? All this beauty that fades and is no more. I never thought of fall as the dying time of year until I came here."

"Aye. Yet unless it dies, it canna be resurrected."

Arthur knew Donald meant more than falling autumn leaves. It wasn't the first time they had spoken on the subject. Living where they did, birth and death surrounded them, more sharp and elemental than in kinder lands. "Sometimes I feel I have died to what I once was," Arthur mused. "If Fa—those back home saw me, I wonder if they would believe a Baldwin could come to this." He held out arms made hard by helping to raise cabins, even as the mountain folk had raised one for him months earlier. He gloried in the fact he could tramp mountains and ford streams without succumbing to exhaustion. One day he would need the strength gained through trudging to patients who lived far from his home. He knew not when or why, just that it was so.

"All these months, ye've kept silent. If ye wish to speak, I weel listen."

Arthur paused for a long time, then haltingly told Donald every sordid detail of his life, all he had glossed over or omitted when speaking of it before. He finished with a plea. "Donald, would you pray for me? Do you think God can forgive me?" He held his breath, eyes burning, afraid to look at his friend for fear of seeing horror in the other's face.

"Dinna ye ken the Father's already forgi'en ye? Why else wud He send His Son, but to take our sins? Laddie, I canna say aught but that." Warm understanding flashed from Donald's eyes. "Ye've kicked agin' the traces and it's brought ye suffering. Now ye must forgi'e the lad ye were."

"That's what Bern's father said. I heard him praying—for me." Arthur had trouble getting it past an obstruction in his throat. "I don't know how he could do it. In his place, I couldn't."

"What did the mon say?"

Word for word it came out, exactly as Arthur heard it from the downcast Benjamin Clifton's lips more than a year earlier. "'And Arthur, who surely is tortured by what he has done. Help him to accept Thy forgiveness and learn to forgive himself.'" He paused, steadied his voice. "He ended by saying, 'Father, into Thy hands I commend my boys. For Jesus' sake.'"

Again the tiny candle of hope he had felt lighted in his aching, repentant heart flickered. "If I had not overheard the prayer, I am not sure what would have become of me."

"Coom." Donald rose and started down toward Arthur's cabin. "Do ye have the Auld Book?"

"No." Arthur quickened his pace to keep up.

"Laddie, how can ye expect to be gi'en guidance wi'out a map?" Donald led the way past several places to his own cabin about a half mile from Arthur's.

The young doctor never forgot the following session. In clear and undeniable terms, the Scotsman showed Arthur the plan of salvation instituted before the beginning of the world. His gnarled fingers nimbly turned to passage after passage. Each message that Jesus took away the condemnation of the world broke a strand in Arthur's chain of guilt.

Many sounded vaguely familiar. Arthur had probably heard them since childhood. Now they came alive, bringing hope and humility. "If God cared that much about me, then I am His," he brokenly said hours later. "I can't imagine why He sacrificed His Son for such as I, but I believe it." A repentant prayer asking for forgiveness and inviting the Lord into his heart left Arthur more at peace than he remembered being in his entire life.

"Ye be a new creature," Donald rejoiced. "Ye are clean as a newborn bairn in the sight of God." His face glowed and he embraced the young man.

"Donald MacDonald, you are a fraud," Arthur exclaimed. "Once I asked if you were a minister and you said no. Why, you're better than any preacher I ever knew or heard about. You should be called Patriarch of the Hollow."

The Scotsman shook his head and replied as he had done so long ago, "Nay. I am only Donal' MacDonal', who loves the Lord and His bairns, young and old." Shaggy white eyebrows met above the keen blue eyes. "Laddie, great is the rejoicing in heaven this day."

"I just wish Bern knew. It might take away some of the bitterness."

"Is he a believer?"

"He used to be," Arthur said wistfully. "Before I . . ." He couldn't go on. "Donald, I'd give my life to find him."

"Canna ye not seek him out?"

"I don't know where he is. I'm not sure even his father knows."

"Send a bit of a letter, laddie, and wait."

❧

A reply came weeks later. Benjamin Clifton rejoiced at Arthur's news but didn't know where Bern was. He promised to write if he got word. Autumn died. Winter raged. The Hollow lay deep in snow, cut off from the outside world.

Doc Noble ran himself ragged—yet the miracle of hope, spring, and the resurrection burned in his heart.

three

Spring 1895 brought joy and tragedy to the Hollow. Arthur's heart swelled along with the dogwoods that burst into waxy white bloom. He experienced a pang every time he saw the gorgeous, pink-adorned redbuds, also called Judas trees. According to legend, Judas Iscariot hanged himself on a redbud tree. Had it been less than two years since Arthur became a Judas? He marveled that the time had passed so easily. Ever since he put aside fairy tales and accepted the true King into his life, he had experienced freedom from searing memories. Deep inside he knew he still must face Bern Clifton, yet much of the dread had vanished.

One day word came from Bern's father. A message had arrived in Philadelphia, telling of the prodigal son's wanderings since he left the home of his father. Bern had wandered for a time, even as Arthur, then headed north instead of south. The scrawled note he sent had been long delayed. By the time it reached Benjamin and he answered, Bern no longer remained in that area. Benjamin's letter came back marked in heavy black letters No Such Person Here.

How bitter Arthur's disappointment! He had been sustained throughout the winter months by his study of the Bible with Donald. But now the goal of his life became to find Bern and witness to him of the life-changing power of the Lord Jesus Christ. The young doctor's spirits drooped low when he read the elder Clifton's closing: *I fear Bern has not forgiven either of us. He did not mention what happened.*

35

Neither did his letter express anything except information obviously given from a sense of duty and because he promised to keep in touch.

A second blow fell while Arthur still reeled with disappointment. Called in to attend a feverish child complaining of headache and stomach pain, he discovered dreaded rose-colored spots on the small chest and abdomen. Typhoid fever! Arthur immediately ordered everyone to boil all water. He sent samples away for testing from the branch and every well. The branch water came back positive, and person after person fell ill from initial contact. A ceaseless round of bathing patients and teaching the strong how to care for the sick without catching the disease left him no time to brood.

Gradually patients improved, yet despite Arthur's working day and night, two of the fifteen who came down with the fever died.

"Why?" he asked Donald, whose red-rimmed eyes showed he had permitted himself no more sleep than the doctor. "I tried just as hard, gave just as good care to those two as the others."

"Ye canna be God, laddie, wi' the power of life and death." Donald sighed. "Dinna fret. Be glad for those ye helped."

"I never felt this way about my patients in Philadelphia." Arthur's shoulders sagged. "I suppose because once I finished in surgery, others took over." He put his tired head down on his folded arms. "My patients here are so much more than gallbladders from Ward 6 or accident victims sent up from Emergency."

"Aye."

"I know now I must leave here, Donald. God's voice seems to be more and more clearly telling me to go. Yet never again will I be satisfied to perform surgery as though a diseased organ is separate from the total person." Arthur stood, stretched, and stumbled toward the door. "I'm going home to rest. Let me know if I'm. . ." A mighty yawn swallowed the last words.

"Aye, laddie." Donald waved him out, then stood for a long time in the doorway of his cabin. Mist like that in his beloved Scotland dells rose to his blue eyes. He watched Arthur until the stumbling figure faded from sight before wearily turning to his bed. "Father, I canna ask the laddie to stay, but I dinna ken what we'll do wi' out him. I weel miss the laddie sore." Exhaustion as much from pending loneliness as worry and hard work fell over Donald like a mantle. Just before he slipped into dreamless sleep, he remembered something that made him smile. Patriarch of the Hollow, the lad had called him. Nay, just Donal' MacDonal,' who served his God through loving the bairns, young and old.

≈

June arrived in shades of pastel. The Great Smokies bloomed into loveliness. Mountain laurel crowded close to the trails. The glossy dark green leaves and pink or white flowers—some marked with purple—added incredible beauty to the woods.

Before another winter, "Doc Noble" must pull up the roots he had sent down and move on. Each visit to a remote cabin, every passing "howdy" on trail or track brought a pang.

Once he told Donald, "I hate partings. One of the things I treasure most about heaven is knowing we will never again have to say good-bye to our loved ones." He took a deep breath, held it, then blew out.

"Aye." Taciturn as ever, the Scotsman kept his own counsel, until a look of naked misery in his face betrayed him.

Arthur didn't let on by the blink of an eyelash that he'd noticed anything amiss. Talking over the upcoming separation would only make things worse.

A transformation began in the young doctor's life and thinking. Part of him clung to each passing day. Yet even though his time of departure loomed uncertainly in the future, he felt a kind of distancing. He could not explain. Neither did he care to discuss it with Donald. "Lord, is this Your way of making things easier?" he prayed one evening at the end of another grueling day. "In some ways, it's as if I've already left the Hollow." His feeling of transition grew, cushioning the actual moment of farewell.

Arthur thought himself prepared because of the strange sense of distance. He discovered how wrong he was when the actual time came. His leaving hadn't been announced. Neither had his actual identity, for Donald had firmly advised against it. "Folks mought wonder," he said. "We'll tell them at the next singing convention ye canna bide wi' us longer."

Arthur enjoyed the all-day singings with "dinner-on-the-grounds." Held on a Sabbath when the circuit rider preached elsewhere, young and old participated. They sang gospel songs in the four-part harmony learned from singing schools conducted when folks had time to attend.

The last delicious crumb of dinner vanished. The final note of "Blest Be the Tie that Binds," sung to close every singing convention, rose to the treetops then winged on up to God's throne. Would Arthur ever forget the last stanza, the verse he could not sing?

When here our pathways part
We suffer mutual pain;
Yet, one in Christ and one in heart,

We hope to meet again.

The desire to cry out that he could not go threatened to overwhelm him. The past two years had intertwined his life with each family present. He felt like a wishbone, pulled two ways until it split into jagged edges.

Donald raised his weathered hand, rough from his service to others. "The Father has seen fit to send our dochtor to bide wi' us this time. He canna stay longer."

Silence gave way to loud cries of protest.

Donald waited then held up his hand. "The laddie has a dooty." He hesitated and looked at Arthur. "To his kinfolk."

Heads wagged. No one cherished family ties more than the listeners. Kinfolk stuck together, often with tragic results. The slightest slur on a family member offered cause for retaliation. While there were no blood feuds in the Hollow, tales of dark deeds that flowed from one generation to the next ran rampant.

At the word *kinfolk,* Arthur's heart leaped. The Cliftons' beloved faces rose in his mind and steeled his determination. But his newfound strength threatened to shred when one of the least-uns tugged on his sleeve. Shining eyes stared out of an anxious face.

"Doc Noble, air ye comin' back? Ain't we never gonna see ye no more?"

Arthur mutely appealed to Donald. The Scotsman stooped, scooped up the urchin in clean but well-patched overalls. "Laddie, he weel coom if he can. We dinna ken that noo. If we see him nae more in the Hollow, we'll meet one day in the Bright Land."

"With Jesus?" the child demanded, giving a little wriggle of anticipation.

"Aye."

Arthur met Donald's level glance above the little one's head—and knew. Although a more formal farewell would take place in Asheville, their true good-byes had just been exchanged.

He managed to get through the welter of good wishes and handshakes, then turned away, heart full. Would he ever again see these backwoods people he loved? Would God in His goodness again guide his steps this way? Long, uncertain years lay between him and such a possibility. If Arthur one day rode back over the hogback, would the old Scotsman stand by his cabin door? Nay. The Patriarch of the Hollow's years were already many. Soon he would follow the last trail and dwell in the Bright Land.

❧

Early the next morning the two companions mounted mules and started up the steep, winding track that led to the crest of the ridge. Arthur reined in his beast on top for a last, soul-filling look. Fall with its increasing chilly nights had painted a world fit for King Midas, the greedy fairy tale monarch who prayed everything he touched would turn to gold. Scarlet thrusts of sumac and the eternal, sentinel-like evergreens spread a living tapestry no artist could surpass. Wispy smoke curled from awakening cabins and lent autumn tang to the clear air.

Too deeply moved for words, Dr. Arthur Baldwin turned away and silently followed Donald MacDonald back toward civilization. The Scotsman would remain in Asheville for a time, again searching for a doctor.

"Donald," Arthur told him. "If you cannot find one, don't grieve too much. You have the skills to do a great deal. I learned that when you kept vigil with me. There's also a chance I can find someone with good skills who didn't graduate in the top class percentage and who wants to get experience." He laughed, a joyous sound in contrast with his heavy heart. "You will have to admit, the Hollow offers endless opportunities to learn!"

"Aye." Donald chuckled and his eyes nearly closed in the wrinkles that formed around his blue eyes. ".He weel nae be you, laddie, but the Father mought have someone in mind."

❧

Long before daylight the next morning, Arthur rose. He had not disrobed the previous night. Neither had he slept. Despite knowing he must go, the niggling fear he would back out if he looked again into the Scotsman's craggy face haunted him. Better to slip out in the murk of dawn. He had taken the precaution to park his bag by the door. Now he noiselessly slid from bed. Shoes in hand, he felt his stocking-footed way across the room, then stooped to gather his bag and open the door.

"Blest be ye, laddie," came a voice from the darkness.

"And you, Donald." Arthur stepped outside. By the dim light of a nearby street lamp he donned his shoes and trudged away, passionately wishing he were going home to a father just like the old man he left behind.

❧

Arthur Baldwin, Junior, reached Philadelphia in a far more prosperous state than when he left. The payment he received from his patients in the Hollow—usually in the form of food—had met his simple needs, and so he had had no need to spend the money from his grandmother's estate. He lingered in Asheville long enough for the banks to open. The quarterly stipends from his inheritance had accumulated and he possessed what appeared to his mountain-trained mind an exorbitant sum of money.

"Funny. Two years ago I'd have spent this much on gambling without a qualm," he mused. A wide grin spread over his tanned face. His blue eyes sparkled. "Anyone needing a change of perspective should go live in the Hollow for a time where cash money is scarcer than frog hair."

He withdrew just enough money to purchase train tickets to Philadelphia and food along the way. The rest he ordered to be transferred back to his old bank. Even if he didn't remain there long, the money would be on hand when he needed it.

Every turn of the wheels that carried him away from North Carolina and back to Pennsylvania brought mixed feelings. He experienced a limbo-like emotion, as if he didn't belong anywhere. No longer part of the Hollow, neither did he feel part of his old world. Perhaps he never would. The cream of Philadelphia would look down its collective nose and consider him quixotic. If he kowtowed to his father and returned to the Baldwin mansion, welcome mats to the best homes in the city would be spread before his unwilling feet, but he wanted no part of the hypocrisy. A few days to see Benjamin Clifton and gain an interview with his own father to learn if any love remained between them—and he'd be off.

The train ride gave him time to meditate. More and more he prayed for reconciliation with his father and thereby his mother. Arthur pictured himself showing them the way of the Cross. His brow wrinkled. They already considered themselves Christians. Could he express their need to know Christ in a personal way without offending them further? He fell asleep to the *clickety-clack, clickety-clack* of the train wheels as they thundered north, still pondering a million questions he had held in abeyance while he lived in the Hollow.

ಎ

Still roughly dressed, Arthur stepped from the train and narrowly avoided an encounter with a group of laughing former acquaintances who were seeing one of their number onto the New York train. He grinned and ducked his head. When in Philadelphia, do as the Philadelphians do had long been the unspoken rule. He didn't care a fig what others thought but reports to Baldwin, Senior, concerning the return of a slovenly son meant death to his hopes of reconciliation. Only to Benjamin Clifton would the long-absent doctor present himself in clothing brought from the Hollow.

Arthur's feet fairly flew over the pavement. This time he did not hesitate at the gate or outside the window. He had sinned grievously, repented, been forgiven by God and Benjamin Clifton. Sure of his welcome, he ran lightly up the walk, tapped at the door, and stepped into outstretched arms.

"Arthur. Arthur, my boy!" Benjamin Clifton said again and again.

In the time that followed, the young doctor sat at the other's table as in days of yore. He hungrily ate the food they worked together preparing. At last, he sank into the chair Benjamin indicated. In response to his host's plea to tell him everything, Arthur said, "It's a long story," and began.

Starting with the moment he left the meeting of the hospital directors bent on forcing him into Bern's rightful place, he talked for hours. Not once did he spare himself or attempt to minimize his wrongdoing. He didn't omit a single detail, including the tiny candle of hope lighted by the prayer of one who never suspected he had been overhead. He told of the Hollow and its people, of Donald and his faith. Last of all, Arthur told how he had confessed his sins and asked

Christ to be King of his life.

"I intend to find Bern and tell him," he finished.

Sadness swept over the older man's lined face. "I pray it may be so but I have heard no more from him. The weeks become months and still no messages come. At times I wonder if the Great North has swallowed my son."

"God knows where Bern is even when we don't," Arthur huskily told him.

"Stay with me while you are here," Benjamin invited. "Unless—" He broke off.

"Thank you, I'd like to stay here. I haven't seen Father. There are things I need to do before contacting him," Arthur said.

A few days later, an impeccably dressed doctor presented himself at his father's house. He knew that appearing like the Biblical prodigal son, fresh from tending the swine, would not have impressed Arthur Baldwin, Senior—but the fact that his only offspring had not only survived but come home strong and unwavering might. To that end, Arthur had sacrificed some of his precious hoard of money for a fine suit of clothing and a visit to a loquacious barber. The man had cut his hair in the latest style, shaved him, and imparted the news of nation, world, and state. How little it interested Arthur! He wondered what the barber would have said if his customer had demanded, "Can you ride a mule, cultivate land, hoe corn? No? Then I'm a better man than you."

Mouth tilted skyward at the corners, Arthur formally lifted the imposing door knocker of the mansion that had never been a home. Slow steps, a fumbling with the door, then it swung in. "Why, Master Arthur!" The butler, to whom the son of the house would always be a child, stared as if he had seen a specter from the great unknown. "Is it really you?"

"Of course. Is Father in?" Arthur stepped into the lavishly decorated hall.

"Y-yes. I'll announce you."

What ailed the man? Had he developed serious illness in the past two years? Keen doctor eyes examined the pasty face and trembling hands. "Are you ill?"

"Why, no." He licked his thin lips. "It's just that—"

"Who is it?" A voice boomed from the open library doors.

Arthur patted the butler's stiffened arm. "I'll announce myself." Long strides took him into the room indelibly etched in his memory from the last time he saw it. The rich oriental rug lay without a wrinkle. Dead ashes filled the hearth. The aroma of a fine cigar hung in the air. Arthur rubbed his eyes. Had he dreamed the last two years?

The elder Baldwin rose from a massive chair and stepped to the exact spot from which he'd hurled his ultimatum: full obedience or banishment. "I knew you'd come crawling back."

four

Arthur Baldwin, Senior, flipped his half-smoked cigar into the fireplace and repeated, "I knew you'd come crawling back." An unpleasant smile rested on his heavy face. "What did you do, find out the magnificent inheritance from your grandmother couldn't even keep you in clean linen? I have to admit, you held out longer than I thought you would."

His son clenched sweaty hands behind him. "I'm not crawling back. I came to see Benjamin Clifton—and you. Mother, as well, if you permit it. I'm leaving Philadelphia again, probably for good."

"Where are you going this time?" Baldwin jeered. "Seems you'd have a bellyful of rebellion after where you've been the past two years. What did those Tarheels do, run you out of the Hollow?"

So he'd cared enough to have his son followed. Why did the thought leave Arthur cold? "I'm heading West." Blue gaze met blue gaze head-on. "I wasn't driven from the Hollow. Every person there begged me to stay but there's something I have to do."

"My son, the hillbilly." Baldwin's voice grated. "Bah, you make me sick. You who could have been somebody, living in a pigsty among dumb—"

Arthur found himself posing the question he'd considered firing off at the sleek barber. "Can you ride a mule? Cultivate land? Hoe corn? I can. Does that make me or those who do so dumb? I chopped wood to earn meals, accepted food instead of money for my services. The best thing you ever did for me was drive me away. It taught me I could make it on my own. I never again need rely on the family name to make my living. I also learned there is honor in any labor, so long as it is honest."

For a moment he felt his father would go into an apoplectic fit. Baldwin's face turned dangerously red, as if sluggish dark blood threatened to burst through his skull. "You insolent whelp! Is that all you came here for?"

Ashamed of his outburst, Arthur said in a low voice, "No, sir. I apologize for my beastly temper." He didn't add "*inherited from you,*" but the unspoken words hung in the air. "I came to tell you I was a fool and worse until I turned my life over to God months ago. Now I'm going to find Bern Clifton and tell him what a terrible thing I did. This is my atonement. God has forgiven me, but I need to do this in order to forgive myself." Arthur took a step toward his father, hoping for a glimmer of understanding in the impassive face. "Will you give me your blessing and let me see Mother?"

For a single heartbeat he thought his father would give in. The next instant scorn swept aside any sign of weakening. "So you've added fanaticism to your insanity." Baldwin swore. "I gave my final word two years ago. I never change, thank God."

"Thank God I have," Arthur quietly replied. He turned to go, miserably aware of how badly he had failed in his mission of reconciliation. He stopped. Must he be sent from his father's presence like a small boy whipped for something he did not do? He turned.

"Father, you have power over many things in my life. You have disinherited me, disowned me as your son. Yet one thing you can never do, in spite of all your wealth and authority. It is something over which you have no control."

"Just what is that?" The disbelieving words flicked like a lash on torn skin.

"You cannot stop my caring what becomes of you." Truth burned within Arthur, bringing a kind of joy holy. He threw off shackles that had bound him for years. With recognition came mastery and the freedom a lifetime prisoner knows when his bonds are removed. "I will pray for you and Mother until the day I die. If it be allowed by my Heavenly Father, I will cry to Him on your behalf with my last breath."

The older man shriveled before the vow. Much of the bombast that allowed him to bully his way through life fled before the candor in his son's radiant face. Unable to speak, Baldwin pointed toward the doorway with a trembling hand, then sank into the chair by the fireplace and turned his head away. His mouth worked but no words came.

"Good-bye, Father. Tell Mother I will write and let you know I am well." Arthur stepped from the cloying atmosphere, feeling he had just won the battle of a lifetime. Certainly, the war to quench his spirit had begun before he graduated from short pants.

"Master Arthur." The butler stood by his side, nervously plucking at Arthur's sleeve, face still pale.

"Yes?"

"I—" The man cast a frightened glance back at the library. "'Twasn't that I was not glad to see you. Orders, y' know." He pressed the back of his hand to his lips and whispered, "It's as good as my place if he hears, but luck to you."

Arthur lowered his voice. "Thank you but I have something far better than luck. I've learned to know God. Good-bye." He smiled and marched out, leaving the gasping butler in the hall. The heavy front door closed with a solid thud, an exclamation point defining the end of another chapter of his life.

Only then did he realize his body was drenched with sweat, heavy as though he'd just helped raise a log cabin back in the Hollow. Yet the strength that came when he gave his own ultimatum sustained him for the long walk back to Benjamin Clifton and acceptance.

❧

One thing remained before Arthur could leave Philadelphia with a clear conscience. The same afternoon his spirit had triumphed over scorn, he began his search for a doctor willing to go to the Hollow. Most of those he approached laughed in his face. All ignored his pleas of how much they were needed and could learn.

Benjamin Clifton shared his struggles. One evening when a dispirited Arthur returned from his fruitless search the older man suggested, "Perhaps you are going about this all wrong. Son, you believe God wants someone in the Hollow to care for His children, don't you?"

"Of course, but He's mighty slow providing. I ran out of names today. Not one showed enough interest to even hear me out." His blue eyes flashed with frustration and anger.

"Would you have done so two years ago?"

The direct challenge snapped the young doctor to attention. He felt a warm red tide sweep into his face. "No." Arthur laughed sheepishly. "I guess it's easy to condemn others for the same failings we possess." He spread his hands wide. A lock of his sunny hair fell over his intelligent forehead. "I just don't know where to go from here."

"Why don't we ask the Great Physician?" Benjamin knelt. When Arthur did the same, the kindly old man prayed earnestly on behalf of those faraway people Arthur had learned to love and appreciate. With a final, "Nevertheless, let it be according to Thy will," he added a quiet amen and rose.

"It's in His hands now. What better place can we leave our perplexities?" He smiled a curious smile. "I am not blessed with the gift of prophecy, yet it won't surprise me if we receive our answer in the most unexpected way. Now, let's consider if there is anything else we can do to get that reply."

"Why—?" Arthur stared.

Benjamin laughed outright. "Just because we leave the final results in the Master's hands doesn't mean we can or should sit back in rocking chairs and do nothing," he pointed out. "After all, God gave us intelligence. Is it any less an answer from Him if it comes through our discovering the paths He has made straight by going before us and preparing the way?"

Day after day they waited. Arthur grew restive but Benjamin's eyes often twinkled. Once he took down his worn Bible and read from the first chapter of James, "*Knowing this, that the trying of your faith worketh patience. But let patience have her perfect work, that ye may be perfect and entire, wanting nothing. If any of you lack wisdom, let him ask of God, that giveth to all men liberally, and upbraideth not; and it shall be given him. But let him ask in faith, nothing wavering. For he that wavereth is like a wave of the sea driven with the wind and tossed. For let not that man think that he shall receive any thing of the Lord.*"

Arthur threw his hands into the air. A rueful smile twisted his lips. "I surrender. I've never been on a ship driven by the wind and tossed but I can imagine it." He thought of great paintings he had viewed, of vessels assaulted and broken. Thankfulness to a God who could calm those stormy seas filled him. "Life has a way of tossing one, doesn't it?"

"Yes." Sadness swept over the other's thin face, honed by those crashing waves experienced by everyone who lives. "All we can do is cling to our faith and not waver." His head bowed. "If I'd had the courage to ride the gale and be honest with my son, he wouldn't be lost to me now." Anguish and regret showed in his bent shoulders, yet the next moment he raised his head and smiled. "Forgive me, as I am still trying to forgive myself."

Arthur soberly told him, "I understand only too well." He straightened and forced cheerfulness into his voice. "Don't forget I am going to find Bern, no matter how long it takes, just as soon as we—no, God—finds a doctor for the Hollow. I pray it will be soon."

Neither Benjamin's prediction nor Arthur's wish came true immediately. Determined not to let themselves grow despondent, the two men continued to pray. They also grew more father-and-son-like than ever. The ever-darkening autumn evenings and an early winter snow that covered Philadelphia with its diamond-studded, ermine cape gave them time for meditation. The companions sought and found a nearby church, in great contrast with the lofty edifice in which the Baldwins worshiped. A minister in a plain business suit preached the gospel straight from the Bible. The power and authority that surrounded him, plus his incredible knowledge of what he called his Guidebook, offered answers to questions that had plagued the new convert. He and Benjamin never tired of hearing the verses concerning forgiveness.

Arthur bypassed medicine to avoid rousing the sleeping

scandal concerning him and found work in building. His apprenticeship in the Hollow served him well. He steadfastly refused to accept Benjamin's hospitality with no return, although the older man protested that Arthur would be using his growing store of funds on the Cliftons' behalf.

"Just keep cooking those wonderful stews and such for when I get home hungry as a calf bawling for her mother," the worker teased. "Besides, I actually enjoy sawing boards and nailing. I'll wager Jesus did, too." A warm feeling curled into his heart like a kitten in his master's lap.

One night at supper Benjamin announced, "I had a visitor today. Our pastor stopped by with a request. He wants to know if you will share how you met the Lord in the Hollow."

Arthur's fork clattered to his plate. "Me? Stand up in front of everyone and speak?"

Benjamin calmly buttered a piece of piping hot cornbread, then remarked, "If you were asked to give a testimonial for a dear friend, would you refuse because you found it too hard to stand up and speak for him?"

Arthur grimaced. "You certainly have a way of shooting holes into a man's excuses, don't you?"

"I?" Benjamin looked innocent but the twitch of his lips gave him away. "All I asked was—"

"I know what you asked and the answer's no. I mean, no I wouldn't refuse and yes, I'll speak." He paused and his brows drew together in a straight line. "I wonder how much I should tell?"

"Son, speak that which the Father puts into your heart and mouth."

Arthur felt a gauntlet had been flung at his feet. Picking it up meant putting full trust in the Lord. He wrestled with the challenge as Jacob once wrestled with an angel—and came out feeling both exhausted and exalted.

"Lead me, Lord," he whispered when the time came and he stepped behind the simple wooden pulpit and looked into the eyes of the expectant congregation. A flash of insight told him they knew exactly who he was. It disconcerted him for a moment. In the weeks he and Benjamin had attended, Arthur had made no effort to identify or deny his connection with the Baldwins. A second bit of knowledge inserted itself into him and he knew what he must do, painful as it might be.

Arthur began by stating how he left Philadelphia more than two years earlier after betraying a friend. He didn't go into details, merely relating he had meant to atone by giving his life in service. His voice strengthened, remembering aloud his rescue by Donald MacDonald, "who loved the Lord and His bairns." Self-consciousness vanished and radiance came until he felt caught up by a power not his own.

"I rode muleback into the Great Smoky Mountains of North Carolina," he said. "I found people living as they have since their ancestors first settled the Hollow. I learned joy does not depend on prestige or might. Cash money is scarce, compassion abundant. The people share what they have. The Hollow is a far cry from heaven, though. There is ignorance, superstition, wariness of strangers. But there is God." He described the meetings, singing conventions, respect for God even among those whose lives fell far short of Christianity. He never knew how long he talked. No one moved restlessly. No impatient feet shuffled.

Last of all, Arthur told them how he found the only way to be free from sin and remorse, the only way to find joy and gladness, in the person of Jesus Christ. "I asked Him to become Ruler of my life," he said. "If I were not committed to a quest, I would have stayed in North Carolina." His wonderful smile widened. "Now I'm waiting for the Lord to help me find a doctor for the Hollow. In the meantime, I'm having to learn patience through waiting on Him!"

A ripple swelled through the congregation and sighs showed others had fought the same battle for patience.

"I just have one thing more to say. I had gone to church since childhood and knew about Jesus. It took tragedy for me to learn to know Him personally." His face shadowed. "If I had, the tragedy would never have occurred." He walked back to his seat and sat down.

Benjamin silently gripped the younger man's hand. Something in his face showed how keenly he longed for the days when he had been a minister. Arthur sensed if reconciliation ever came between Clifton and his son, the man beside him would again feel free to speak for his Lord. He vowed again that if it were in his power to find Bern Clifton, he would do so.

After the final hymn and benediction, worshipers crowded around the tall, fair man and his companion. Men gripped their hands. Sincere thanks poured into Arthur's ears. A middle-aged man stood apart, obviously waiting for the crowd to thin. At last only he, Benjamin, Arthur, and the minister remained.

"Young man, you are an answer to prayer." Keen black eyes matched the dark streaks in the stranger's salt-and-pepper hair. He gripped Arthur's hand in a clasp that made the young doctor wince. "For the last six months I've known the Lord had a work for me. Hang it all, I haven't been able to discover what or where it was." He paused significantly. "Until today."

Arthur's mouth fell open. Did this mean what it sounded like?

"I believe God sent you here today. I am Dr. Aldrich, sick of cities and rich patients whose ailments could be cured by less self-indulgence and more common sense." His intense gaze never left Arthur's face. "My world crashed a year ago when my wife died. We never had children." He inhaled sharply then sighed. "I threw myself heart and soul into my practice and grew more disgusted and miserable every day. Volunteering in the poorer sections of the city salved my conscience, yet for some reason it wasn't the answer."

"You believe the Hollow is." Arthur's heart pounded with joy.

"I do." Dr. Aldrich's eyes glistened. "How do I go about becoming the Hollow's physician? Is your cabin available? Will the mountaineers accept me?"

"Aye, you will be wi' Donald MacDonald." Arthur didn't realize he had dropped into dialect until Dr. Aldrich burst into delighted laughter. He joined in the fun at his expense. "If the cabin's occupied, they and you will build another. Can you ride muleback? Help cultivate land? Hoe corn? Acceptance depends on how quickly you adapt to the way of life in the Hollow."

"Could you do those things when you got there?" Dr. Aldrich challenged.

Arthur shook his head vigorously. "Many a blister adorned these hands before they became callused," he confessed. "By the way, mutton tallow's good for cracked hands."

The black eyes twinkled. "You young upstart, I've been a doctor since before you got out of diapers. Don't be prescribing for me!" Merriment gave way to interest. "Mutton tallow. Hmm. Not a bad idea."

Arthur enthusiastically burst out, "I can hardly wait to send word to Donald!" He laid his hand on the other doctor's sturdy shoulder. "There will be times you may wonder what you are doing there. I did. You'll fight superstition and tradition as well as disease—and you'll be discouraged."

"Are you trying to talk me out of going?" Dr. Aldrich bluntly demanded. "Save your breath. After this morning, nothing can convince me God isn't calling me to the Hollow." His lips slitted into a seam. "I shudder to think how nearly I didn't attend church this morning. My maid spilled boiling water on her hand minutes before time for me to leave. By the time I dressed the burn and administered something to quiet her, time had flown. I hate being late and considered staying home, but my carriage had already been brought around."

Arthur felt compelled to add, "I also came on unwilling feet." He told how he had struggled with the invitation to speak. "Dr. Aldrich, it will take some time for me to get a message through to Donald. You'd do well to settle up your business here in Philadelphia and plan to go to the Hollow in spring."

"I shall. God bless you in your quest." If the sharp-eyed physician discerned what that quest might be, he kept it to himself. "Young man, if our paths don't cross again here, we'll meet again. Someday." Another bone-crushing grip of Arthur's strong hand and Dr. Aldrich strode out of the church.

"He will do well," Benjamin softly said.

"Aye." Something Donald had said long ago sang in Arthur's brain. *He will nae be you, laddie, but the Father mought have someone in mind.*

Filled to overflowing, Arthur gave thanks. That someone had been found.

five

Inga Nansen turned from the beckoning waters of Puget Sound and resolutely faced the city of Seattle. Bleeding inside at the thought of separation from the father she loved second only to God, she held her head high and squared her shoulders. A sob escaped her tightly compressed lips and she clenched hands made strong by shipboard duties. Lars Nansen, who could spot a treacherous reef or shallow bar long before most of the sailors on the *Flower of Alaska*, must not see her cringe.

Her ears told her when the ship steamed out of the Sound. Still she did not look back. To do so would be to break faith. "God," she whispered. "Go with Him and stay with me." Comfort stole into her aching heart.

She pulled her cloak close against the wind coming in off the Sound. Tall, strong and upheld by generations of sturdy, Scandinavian stock, more than ever she resembled some glorious figurehead on a Viking ship. Inga shook tears from her fjord-blue eyes and with long strides, climbed the steep hills that led from the docks to the city perched above her like a great, hovering bird.

Miles lay between her and the University of Washington. She didn't care. The long walk would give her a time of transition. The *Flower of Alaska* was no longer home. But neither was the comfortable room in a private house near the university, one of those on the school's highly recommended list for those who wished to live with a family.

The thought of actually being landlocked for months and years sent a shiver of panic down the girl's back. Lars, the sailors, earth, sky, and sea had been her family. How would it seem to be around two small children, to be everlastingly shut up in buildings, when her heart, mind, and soul longed for freedom?

She increased her pace, unconscious of the admiring looks cast her way. Inga's buttoned shoes and effortless walk swallowed up distance like big fish swallowing little ones. She reached the tree-lined avenue that would be her home for the next four years. "Nay," she exclaimed. "Three."

She had not told her father, but she intended to complete her education in three years by taking extra courses. Shortly after her twenty-first birthday, she would be free as the mournful gulls crying in the sky above her. Armed with diploma and a degree she never intended to use, once more Inga would feel the roll and pitch of the *Flower of Alaska's* deck beneath her feet and be lulled to sleep by its motion.

Thoughts of the future sustained Inga through matriculation and getting settled. She clung to it when homesickness attacked like a storm at sea. Churning inside, she rode its troughs and valleys until at last it subsided into a distant murmur. Three things helped. The family with whom she lived adored her. She returned their feelings with full devotion and never tired of hearing the children's merry laughter. Gretchen and young Jimmy begged for stories and got them. If their parents had permitted it, they would have made her their willing slave.

The third factor was a cheerful, round-faced college freshman named Sally who also roomed and boarded with the Graysons. It never appeared to enter her head Inga might not want her around constantly. Except for when they were studying, Sally parked on her new friend's bed and curled up kittenlike. Inga soon grew used to having her there, and for the first time she giggled with another girl while pressing the starched shirtwaists she wore to class.

Sally frankly confessed herself a confirmed romantic who had come to college for one year only and with a single goal: to catch a man. "I come from a town so small you're an old maid if you aren't married by the time you're fifteen," she exaggerated. Her round blue eyes twinkled. "Isn't it lucky I found him the first week?" Laughter spurted, so contagious Inga smiled in sympathy.

"Talk about fate, or the mysterious ways God works! Even my wildest imaginings didn't include having such a wonderful man as Dick there to pick me up when I fell down those steep stairs coming from my history class."

Inga had heard the story several times before. Each time Dick became a bigger hero. "I still think you fell on purpose."

"Why, how can you say that?" Sally looked astonished. The next minute her infectious laugh came again. "Not that I wouldn't have, if I'd known Dick would be the one at the bottom, but I couldn't so I didn't."

"You are hopeless!" Inga set her iron down with a thump and hung the warm blouse on a hook ready for the next day's wearing. She'd already brushed down her long dark skirt.

"No, I'm in lo-o-o-ve." Sally pressed both hands to her heart, closed her eyes in rapture, then opened them wide. "Wait 'til it happens to you."

Shivers went through Inga. She pushed aside Sally's wide skirts and curled up next to her, feeling like a mother hen with one fractious chick. "Sally, how can you be so sure, so soon? It's only been a few weeks. You could be mistaken."

A tender expression crossed the smaller girl's face. "No. Something in here says it's right." She laid a hand over her heart. "Besides, we like all the same things—small towns and farms and animals and big families. I'm glad Dick's a senior. We're going to get married as soon as he graduates." She clasped her hands. "He is also a real Christian. I couldn't marry someone who isn't."

"Neither could I." Inga remembered how many times she had gazed into the heavens from the *Flower of Alaska* and marveled that a God so great as to create such wonder yet cared enough for her to sacrifice His only Son.

"If you'd give the young men a chance, they'd be lined up on your doorstep," Sally observed. "Dick says half the senior men would like to call on you but you're so direct, they don't know how to approach you."

"I can't be all maidenly giggles and blushes," Inga retorted, although she felt warm color come into her face. "You aren't either. You just pretend."

Sally grinned. "I'm a reformed woman. Dick doesn't like prattle."

"Oh, dear." Inga gave a mock sigh. "I can see it all now. You'll be one of those 'my husband says this' and 'my husband does that' wives without an opinion on anything."

"I will not!" Sally indignantly sat up. "Why, Dick says one of the things he likes best about me is that I have a mind of my own and speak what I think."

Inga's mirth bubbled over. "*Dick says*? You're quoting him again, Sally."

"You're dreadful, Inga Nansen." Sally snatched a pillow and threw it at her friend before subsiding into a laughing heap. "If you weren't my best friend I'd—I'd—just wait. One of these days you'll be running to me for comfort."

"The Nansens ride their own storms," Inga proudly told her. She softened when she noticed Sally's mouth quivering like a rejected child's. "I can't imagine anyone better able to give comfort than you. Dick has chosen wisely and so have you. You will have a blessed marriage. Perhaps one day I will, too."

Trouble vanished from her friend's face as fog before the sun. "There just might be another man in the world as wonderful as Dick. If there is, I'm sure God has him already picked out and saved for you."

A lump formed in Inga's throat. "I hope so." Unaccustomed melancholy darkened the blue of her eyes. Was there even now someone, somewhere searching just for her? Would she one day tell him she knew he'd come, that she'd waited for him?

❧

Inga continued to wonder all winter while she studied hard and watched Sally and Dick radiate joy despite the sometimes dismal weather. Yet that certain someone did not appear—or if he did, Inga didn't recognize him. She entered wholeheartedly into parties and plays, musicales and debates, yet remained heart-whole, even though several members of the male sex attempted to change her mind. She serenely went her own way and kept her counsel. Not one of the men who sought her favor could compare with Captain Lars Nansen.

Spring arrived in a wealth of blossoming rhododendrons and wild flowers. The campus bloomed into beauty. Inga, Sally, and the other girls packed away dark skirts and shirtwaists. Out came fluffy cotton dresses, pastel lawn, and muslin. Sally favored pink, Inga blue or white.

Despite her height and strength, Inga had a certain

daintiness. She loved a frill here, a bit of lace there, and she set out each morning immaculately attired. Lars had taken her to a good clothing store before she entered school. Consultation with a motherly department head wise enough to see Inga's possibilities had led to a complete, tasteful outfit. Only once had the girl balked.

"Father, what on earth will I do with three evening dresses?" she had protested, hands on her hips.

"Begging your pardon, Miss Nansen, but you will need them for balls," their helpful saleslady put in.

"I do not attend balls."

Something in her tone silenced the automatic protest, and the woman hastily said, "For special class events and dinners, then."

Still doubtful, Inga caught her father's nod and reluctantly tried several gowns. She quickly laid aside all but those with the most modest decolletage and settled on a simple dark blue velvet for winter, a frothy pastel blue and an exquisite lacy white for spring. She knew how becoming they were even more by her father's quick intake of breath than from her mirrored reflection.

"The white's pretty enough for a wedding gown," the saleswoman commented. Inga felt color rise into her face, but she only winked at Lars.

The wardrobe had proved more than adequate. Inga wore the midnight blue velvet several times that winter and Sally begged her to wear the light blue for a maid of honor dress. "Dick and I don't have much money," she frankly said one late spring evening. She sat curled up in her usual position on Inga's bed. "We'll be married in the college chapel." She sounded wistful. "I want to be married in a white dress but I haven't found one I like that I can afford. Do we have time to make one? It would be cheaper."

"Yes, but. . ." Inga's heart pounded. Sally had given her so much friendship, she'd despaired of ever repaying her. Now she had a chance. She ran to her closet and pulled out a satin-lined box. Opening it carefully, she shook out the gorgeous white gown she had never worn. "This is an early wedding present."

Sally gasped and sat up. Her round eyes looked enormous in her shocked face. "You can't mean it!" Delight and disbelief mingled in her expression.

"Of course I mean it. I can't think of anything I'd rather give you." Inga draped the dress over one arm and hauled Sally off the bed with the other. "It should fit perfectly except for the length. I can shorten it, although I have to warn you, the last thing I mended was a torn sail!"

Sally didn't answer.

Inga looked at her friend. Her heart sank. "Don't you like it? If not, I'll buy you one you do. No bride should be anything except proud on her wedding day."

Sally flew to her. Two arms went around Inga and squeezed hard. "Like it! Inga Nansen, that is the most beautiful dress in the whole world. I never dreamed I'd have anything like it in my whole life."

Inga felt hot tears splash on her hand. She shakily ordered, "Then don't cry all over it, you little goose."

Sally backed away and examined the exquisite gown. "I didn't hurt it, did I?"

"No. After the wedding you can take off some of the lace trim and wear the dress for special occasions," Inga suggested.

A rich blush colored Sally's pretty face. "Never," she vowed. "I'm going to save it for my daughter and her daughter to wear on their wedding days and I will never,

ever forget you and what you've done. Oh, Inga, if it weren't for Dick, I couldn't bear to think of leaving you."

The heartbroken cry reached to the core of the other girl's being. What would school be like next year without Sally? Could anyone take her place? Inga shook her head. No, but perhaps God would send someone to create a place of her own and fill the emptiness Inga could already feel growing inside her.

➣

A few weeks later she valiantly held back tears and watched Dick and Sally join their lives in a simple but moving ceremony. Dick had graduated with honors and accepted an accounting job in a small town about twenty miles from Seattle. "Close enough so both you and my folks can come see me," Sally happily chattered. She had never been more attractive than in the white gown. She turned, flung her bouquet of roses straight toward Inga, then threw herself into her friend's arms. "I'll never forget you. Thank you, for everything."

Thank you, Sally, Inga's heart whispered. She dared not prolong the farewell. "Dick is waiting," she reminded. "Godspeed, Sally."

"And to you." The bride turned to her new husband with such a look of love Inga's eyes stung. When would her own someday come?

➣

Summer stretched long and lonely without Sally. No one came to occupy her room until fall, and then Miss Perkins proved a poor substitute for the lovable girl who had left the Grayson household. She taught primary children at a nearby school and showed little interest in anything or anybody else. Inga privately wondered if the new roomer felt it sinful to smile and laugh. She seldom did either.

"We can't just ask her to leave, when she pays regular and doesn't complain on the food," Mrs. Grayson confided in a low whisper. She brightened and patted Inga's hand with her own workworn one. "At least, we still have you. The Good Lord knows how glad we are."

Inga's heart warmed to her landlady. "I am also thankful," she whispered back. "I wonder why Miss Perkins always looks so sad. I can't just ask."

Mrs. Grayson shook her head. "She wears a keep-out sign on her heart, doesn't she? Say, would you like gingerbread for dinner? I have some good soured milk."

Inga readily agreed. She also took extra pains afterward to be pleasant to her fellow guest, whom the—young Graysons disrespectfully called Perky behind her back. Yet the teacher remained an enigma.

The brightest spots on Inga's horizon came with the infrequent arrivals of the *Flower of Alaska*. Lars could never stay long and the poignancy in two pair of blue eyes silently shouted that every parting grew harder. Inga always heaved a great sigh of relief to discover the same steady father she loved. In turn, she knew he offered prayers of gladness she still kept her plaits and had not tortured her hair into one of the styles of the day.

Wrapped up in seeing him, she scarcely noticed someone else also began to anticipate the Captain's visits. She did notice Miss Perkins had begun to spruce herself up and act a little more friendly.

"When is your father coming for another visit?" she inquired one spring day in Inga's second year at the university. "I thought I would ask him a bit about the sea. My pupils are quite interested."

"If you ask me, the only pupils interested are the ones in her eyes," Mrs. Grayson told Inga later. "She's set her cap for the Captain. Not that it'll do her any good. He's polite, 'cause that's his way, but he's not for her."

Inga's mouth fell open. Father and Perky? She couldn't imagine anything more preposterous. Forewarned, she quietly observed Perky's nervous attempts to talk with Lars when he came. She never failed to appear when he did, always with questions that required time-consuming answers. She also added a little bow to her starched shirtwaist whenever the *Flower of Alaska* sailed into the Sound.

Annoyance gave way to pity for the lonely spinster and tenderhearted Inga hatched a plan to save Miss Perkins from inevitable heartache. "Father, don't you think it would be a good idea for us to invite everyone aboard the *Flower of Alaska* before you sail this next time?" she proposed the next time he came.

Captain Lars cocked his head. "Any special reason?"

"The Graysons are very good to me. The children would love seeing the ship and I'm sure Miss Perkins would find it enlightening." Inga paused and tried to look innocent. She didn't intend to plant ideas in her father's head. "A steamship really is interesting, you know, especially the captain's quarters. Most people would never suspect how snug and comfortable they are, with built-in bunks, lockers, even a place for yours and Mother's picture."

Did the shrewd eyes see right through her little scheme? Inga never knew. Lars slowly said, "I sail day after tomorrow. We'll invite them for tomorrow night. The fare won't be like Mrs. Grayson's but I'll manage to come up with something so you won't be ashamed of me."

"Nonsense! I've been itching to get into the galley. I'll do you proud."

True to her word, Inga served the Captain and his guests a simple, but well-prepared meal the next evening with fresh salmon steaks as the main feature. Apple pie worthy of even Mrs. Grayson's best efforts ended the meal, then the children clamored to "see everything."

Through skillful maneuvering on Inga's part, she managed to have Perky enter the Captain's quarters after the others had gone. Inga knew the exact moment when Miss Perkins' gaze fell on the photograph next to her father's bunk, placed where he could see himself and the laughing girl when he awakened.

A certain stillness came to the older woman. "Your mother and father?"

"Yes." Inga's tender heart twisted with sympathy for the pain in the question.

"Did he love her very much?"

"Next to God." The words *so much he has never looked at another woman*, hung unspoken in the quiet cabin.

"She is lovely. You are like her." Miss Perkins turned from the photograph, eyes misty. "I pray you will find a good man, one like your father, who will bring you great happiness." The first real smile Inga had ever seen her wear glorified her plain face. "Captain Lars reminds me of someone I loved before I came to Seattle. We were to be married but he drowned saving a little child. Even though I knew I would meet him in heaven, I couldn't put aside my grief. Seeing your father reminded me John would not want me to mourn and be sad." She touched the brave bow on the starched shirtwaist covering a heart Inga realized ached with every pulsing beat.

To Miss Perkins's utter amazement, the younger woman

threw her arms around her. Never again would she secretly call Miss Perkins Perky. How often had Father warned her not to judge others. Miss Perkins had suffered in silence, needing help but unable to reach out. Suppose it were Inga, mourning her father. Could she gather the remnants of her world and go on as the other had been forced to do?

Inga brokenly cried, "Miss Perkins, did anyone ever tell you what a beautiful person you are?"

The lonely teacher gently stroked the sunny head against her shoulder and softly said, "Only John and the little children. God willing, that will change one day."

six

Those few revealing moments in Captain Nansen's quarters aboard the *Flower of Alaska* won Miss Perkins a place in Inga's sympathetic heart. The day after the dinner aboard the steamship, Inga had a long talk with motherly Mrs. Grayson that resulted in a complete change of attitude. The teacher opened like a slow-blooming rosebud. When her landlady chastised the children for calling their boarder Perky, Miss Perkins only laughed. "I'm afraid Perky doesn't fit me very well. My first name is Ruth, but it would be nice if the children called me Auntie."

"All right, Auntie Perky," Gretchen and young Jimmy solemnly agreed. Mr. and Mrs. Grayson shook their heads in despair over their young ones but again Miss Perkins laughed, a joyous sound that brought life and color to her face.

Spring blossomed into summer and all thought of wanting a different boarder for the next year fled. Instead, Inga and the Graysons discovered that a remarkably intelligent and well-informed person lived in their midst. Ruth, as the adults called her, dropped bits and pieces of information at the dinner table and roused curiosity to know more. She also lent a hand in the kitchen when Mrs. Grayson didn't feel well and begged to take the children on little excursions to park and lakes. Inga usually accompanied them, amazed at the change in the formerly drab woman. Miss Perkins didn't burst out into wild colors but always a bright bow adorned her starched white shirtwaists and when hot days came, she changed to thin gowns of pale lilac or white.

In spite of the outings and rare visits with Sally and Dick, Inga felt herself marking time. Each summer day brought her closer to her third and final year of college. She still hadn't told her father how hard she had studied and that she would complete her course in three years. He knew she had fine reports and stood near the head of her class, although Inga cared little for such honors. Father had sent her to the university to learn and learn she would. While others frivoled away the warm days, she studied as she had the summer before.

Because of her high grades, the university agreed if she could pass several stiff exams when she returned in the fall, they would exempt her from having to take certain classes. Inga knew her dream lay within reach. Spring 1900 promised graduation and freedom. She would miss the Graysons, Sally, Ruth Perkins, and a few others, yet not for a million dollars would she stay one minute longer in Seattle than absolutely necessary. If only the days would go faster, instead of limping like a crippled ship trying to reach the shore before it foundered!

This second summer, though, brought some release from Inga's longing for the *Flower of Alaska*. Near the end of August, the parents of two of the college students at the church Inga faithfully attended moved to a home on the shores of Lake Washington. They promptly invited the entire Christian Endeavor society for a boating party.

Inga smiled to herself but refrained from comparing the flat-bottomed rowboats with sailing on the open sea. She delighted in taking the oars and scooting the boat through the water with powerful strokes, despite protests from the natty gentlemen of the party. More than one of the male escorts admiringly watched the strong girl in her simple white duck skirt and plain white blouse, pink and white face alight with joy.

"Inga, be my partner in the canoe races, will you?" a fellow student called.

"No, mine!" others shouted.

Her eyes glistened. "I'll go with Fred. He asked first." She gracefully stepped into the swaying canoe and grasped a paddle. It felt good in her hands, like an old friend not seen for too long. When Captain Lars had the *Norseman* in drydock for necessary repairs, he and his daughter had explored by canoe the streams and lakes in the area.

Seattle sunlight, brilliant from the reflection of sky and lake, flashed on Inga's gleaming paddle. In, out. In, out. The canoe surged forward, leaving the contenders far behind. She laughed when she saw that Fred, skilled as he was, had trouble matching her strong strokes. She could feel the glow of happiness being on the water always brought and she laughed again, a silver trill fitting the sparkling day.

They rounded the designated turning point and started back, meeting already-defeated contestants who loudly informed Fred he had an unfair advantage in Inga. The young man merely smirked and kept paddling.

Halfway back to the starting point, Inga's ocean-trained eyes caught sight of an unattended child standing on a boat dock directly across from their course. Chubby hands clasped before him, the small boy stood watching the swiftly moving canoe. Inga felt alarm stir. Where were his parents? Why had he been left alone on the dock?

"Change course," she instructed Fred in a voice made tense by fear.

"Why-what—?" He raised his paddle in astonishment,

then did as told. Swift strokes sent them shooting through the water directly toward the boy.

Too late. With a little crow of delight and a clearly audible, "Me swim!" the boy gave a leap that took him away from the safety of the dock and plunged him headfirst into the lake.

"Come as fast as you can," Inga ordered. She stood, snatched off her long skirt and petticoats, took a sighting on where the child had gone down, and dove into the lake. Hampered by shoes she had no time to discard, she whispered a prayer for help and struck out on the shortest course possible. The child bobbed to the top, opened his mouth to cry, and sank again, choking and white-faced.

Horror lent wings to Inga's body. *God, help!* she silently cried, knowing she must save every breath for the rescue. An eternity later she reached the spot she thought he had gone down. Not a ripple marred the water except for the waves her white-clad arms made. She paused, filled her lungs, and dove. Down, down, until she reached the bottom. Thank God the water wasn't so deep here!

Her searching gaze saw nothing. Lungs bursting with the need for air, Inga surfaced and dove again. This time she found a huddled heap on the floor of the lake. She laced the fingers of her left hand in the child's blouse. A series of mighty scissors kicks and frantic stroking with her free hand brought her up like a great, leaping fish.

Incomparable joy filled her. The canoe rocked near, a pale-faced Fred holding it steady with his paddle while he reached a hand down to them.

"Take the child," she called, treading water. "I'll swim to the dock." Minutes later Inga and Fred had the little boy face down on the dock, forcing air into his lungs. He retched a stream of lake water, opened his eyes, and weakly struggled against their ministrations.

"Mama?" His thin wail pierced the air.

A rush of feet brought a terrified woman bounding onto the dock. "Baby?" She reached the three disheveled persons. "Dear God, *what happened?* I only left him for a moment. Does he need a doctor?" She caught him to her breast.

"He tried to swim," Fred huskily told her. "He's all right now but if it hadn't been for Inga. . ." His unspoken words told the rest of the story.

"No," Inga softly said. "I couldn't have done it. God saved your child, not I." She grew conscious of the fact she stood before them clad in long cotton drawers and a shirtwaist that clung like a second skin. "Fred, would you hand me my clothing, please?" Inga felt her skin scorch with shame, but her racing partner's look of admiration for her deed reassured her. She'd wager the *Flower of Alaska* he hadn't paid one whit of attention to her immodest garb.

"Come up to the house and let me dry your clothes," the boy's mother insisted, but Inga shook her head and slipped into her skirt. No sense getting her petticoat soaked, as well.

"Thank you, but no." She pointed to several canoes heading their way. "The others are coming and will worry. I can get dried off at our host's home."

"How can I ever repay you? What is your name? My husband will want to—"

"By never leaving him again, not for a single moment." Inga smiled but her blue eyes remained serious. "Teach him to swim. I learned before I was half his age." She paused, then shyly added, "Be grateful to the Father who saved him."

"I will," the mother fervently promised. She cuddled the tired little boy even closer. Great drops fell on his tear-stained face.

"Put him to bed and let him rest," Inga said. Her sweet smile offered reassurance. "He will be fine in the morning." She and Fred seated themselves in the canoe and she picked up her paddle, shivering in spite of herself. "Ugh, I'm clammy all over. Let's go."

Blanket-wrapped, blonde hair towel-dried and plaited, Inga refused to allow the incident to spoil the outing. Neither would she stand for too much praise. Yet her deed did not go unnoticed. A few days later the Seattle Times carried the story on the front page. The headline read: UNIVERSITY OF WASHINGTON STUDENT SAVES PROMINENT FAMILY'S ONLY CHILD. A remarkably accurate account followed, praising Inga for her courageous action and accompanied by a picture an enterprising reporter had begged, borrowed, or stolen from college records.

The campus went wild. Not often did one of their own receive such good publicity. Inga smiled and gave credit where it belonged, even when the grateful father and mother sent baskets of flowers and fruit that filled every room at the Graysons's. "It's rather sad," she reflectively told Ruth Perkins. "With God's help, I saved one child. He stands ready to save an entire world, through the gift of His Son, and many pay no attention." She sighed. "It's like people worshiping a tool, instead of the One who uses it to accomplish His purposes."

"When the university opens again, the furor will settle down," Ruth predicted.

It did, but only when something new and unexpected took its place. In early October, one of Inga's professors fell ill and a new man came. Professor Byron Irving hit the leaf-strewn campus like a typhoon, fluttering female hearts the way a capricious wind sets golden maple leaves dancing. His flashing dark eyes, tossing black mane, and flowing ties gave him a romantic resemblance to Lord Byron, the idol for whom he had been named.

Even Inga admitted his charm. Raised on the classics, she thrilled when he quoted from them, especially one stanza of Byron's, "Childe Harold's Farewell to England." She and her father knew it by heart and loved it.

" 'Let winds be shrill, let waves roll high, I fear not wave nor wind: Yet marvel not, Sir Childe, that I am sorrowful in mind; For I have from my father gone, a mother whom I love, And have no friends, save these alone, But Thee—and One above.' "

Inga's heart lurched when she heard the familiar words, spoken in a deep voice that held a timbre born by of a passion for poetry unknown to many who taught it. Even more than Byron's works, Inga loved to hear the professor quote Robert Louis Stevenson's poignant "Requiem." It never failed to bring tears.

" 'Under the wide and starry sky, Dig the grave and let me lie: Glad did I live and gladly die, And I laid me down with a will. This be the verse you grave for me: Here he lies where he long'd to be; *Home is the sailor, home from the sea, And the hunter, home from the hill.*' "

Used to adulation, Professor Irving seldom found it grounded in what he taught rather than in himself. Inga's eager face and grasp of concepts offered a challenge not often evident in his students' faces. October drifted into November, and Irving discovered himself looking more and more to the listening young woman for approval. A flash of recognition, a raised eyebrow, the pursing of her mobile mouth fascinated the jaded professor. He asked her to stay after class on the slightest pretense. At last he invited her to attend a poetry reading in a circle composed mainly of other professors. If she passed the test—and he suspected she would—Inga Nansen would be a fitting companion for his leisure hours, at least while he remained at the university.

Inga prepared for her evening with unusual care. During the interval between receiving the invitation and the actual event, she found herself dissatisfied with all the pretty clothes in her wardrobe. "They make me look so schoolgirlish," she complained to Ruth Perkins. "The reading's to be at one of the professor's homes and everyone there will be older."

"You are still a schoolgirl," Ruth quietly reminded her.

"I know, but Professor Irving is thirty, at least. I don't want to embarrass him." She glanced in the mirror and eyed her plaits with disfavor. Hot color poured into her face. "Perhaps I should cut my hair."

"Don't you dare!" Ruth ordered in an unusually sharp tone.

Inga whirled in surprise. "Why, Ruth!"

Pale pink touched the white cheeks. "I don't mean to be domineering but you mustn't change yourself to please any man, although I once did that very thing."

Inga forgot her worries and plopped onto her friend's bed. "Was it John?"

A reminiscent smile curved the thin lips. "Oh, no. Just a new boy in high school I admired from the time he came. He asked a friend about me and learned I had no beau at the time." She blushed. "I'd never been more twittery than when he shyly approached me and asked if he could walk me to a church social the next week."

"What did you do?" Ruth's confession fascinated her listener.

"Fretted and stewed and wanted to buy a complete new wardrobe. He appeared so suave and debonair I wondered why he had ever asked a little nobody like me. I decided to do something to make myself more attractive and like other girls he surely had escorted." She laughed and fun danced in her eyes. "I made over a dress into a more sophisticated style, cut my bangs and frizzed them until I looked like Meg March in *Little Women* after Jo burned her hair."

"What happened?" Inga could almost see plain little Ruth Perkins fixing herself up for a beau.

"I was all set to impress him. I did, all right! He came, was polite as Sir Galahad, and I knew he'd not be back."

"But why?" Inga couldn't understand. "After you went to all that trouble."

"That *was* the trouble!" Ruth sighed, then laughed. "He told my friend afterwards, 'I couldn't believe it. I liked her simple dresses and hairstyle. Why did she change? Now she's just like everyone else.'"

Inga digested the story. "You think Professor Irving asked me to the reading because I'm different?" She cocked her head to one side and waited.

"I don't know. I do know when we try to be someone other than who God intends, we end up not knowing exactly who we are." She patted Inga's hand and smiled. "Wear something pretty, and concentrate on having a good time." She surveyed the younger woman. "If you like, we can do your hair a different way that won't require cutting, frizzing, or torturing."

"All right, but I still think I'll get a new dress. Will you come with me?"

"Of course." Pleasure shone in Ruth's eyes.

They found the perfect dress in the first store they

visited—a rich, sea-blue silk with a creamy lace collar. Inga felt totally elegant without being overdressed.

Ruth proved herself skillful at hair arranging, as well. On Saturday morning, Inga washed her hair early so it would be sure to dry. Instead of plaiting it, Ruth divided the heavy golden mass with a soft center part. She drew the sides back with sparkling combs and coiled it in a loose chignon at the base of Inga's white neck. Neat and tidy, it gave the excited girl a madonnalike look.

Inga twisted her head to better see herself. "I wonder if he will like it."

Ruth wisely made no attempt to answer. The sound of voices in the lower hall brought color to Inga's face and her friend caught up a long, warm cloak. "Wear this," she advised. "It's cold tonight."

Inga looked at her doubtfully. "Shouldn't I just carry it downstairs? I hate to cover up my pretty dress."

"He will see you when you arrive. Now, hold your head up and walk proud."

"Like my father's daughter?" Her eyes looked like two stars beneath a golden crown of hair, dream-filled and eager.

"Like your Heavenly Father's daughter." Ruth followed her charge downstairs, half regretting she had encouraged Inga to set aside her plaits for the evening. Unspoiled by familiarity with the opposite sex, the girl she'd learned to love retained a childlike innocence. God grant she might not lose it. Inga's very belief in the goodness of people made her vulnerable, open to hurt from those who did not maintain her high standards.

Untroubled by such misgivings, Inga set out with Professor Irving. A strange new thrill went through her when he helped her into a carriage. She was used to attentions from boys her own age. This was different. For the first time she found herself disturbed by a man's nearness, and the look she'd seen in his eyes when she first came downstairs.

The evening took on a fairy-tale atmosphere. When they reached their destination, she surrendered her cloak to a waiting maid and turned to her escort. If she lived to be a hundred she wouldn't forget the blaze of admiration in his black eyes. It reassured her, gave her confidence, and from that moment on, the evening was hers. She joined in the discussion as unself-consciously as though she had been a member of the exclusive group for years. Several times she suggested a fresh slant to some phrase. When complimented, she frankly said, "I can't take credit for that. My sea captain father taught me. My name means 'daughter of a hero,' you know."

Those present marveled. Not one of them would have admitted such a relationship in present company. Inga's willingness to do so intrigued them. "She is as Nathanael in the Bible," one muttered. "Utterly without guile." He cast an anxious glance at Inga and the professor. "I hope Irving doesn't change her."

At that moment the professor whispered, "You must call me Byron." The blush and confusion he expected didn't materialize. Inga simply smiled and thanked him. Irving delightedly revised his opinion of her poise. He certainly must cultivate this astonishing creature. Inga had stepped into the hallowed ranks and captivated those present with a manner natural and invigorating as an ocean breeze.

seven

Am I in love?

The question Inga dared not ask aloud quivered in heart and mind. With every passing day, Professor Irving—Byron, she called him outside of class—paid her such marked attention campus gossip had them engaged in a matter of weeks. Yet little things troubled Inga. Although Byron expressed a desire to be in her company as much as possible, not one word of love passed his smiling lips. Perhaps he felt it too soon to declare himself. She appreciated the fact he attempted no further liberties after he had tried to embrace her once and she stepped back. Lars Nansen had instilled in his daughter the desire to keep her lips for the man she married. Would that man be Byron?

The thought sent rich blood to her white brow. It soon faded. What did a professor whose only love for the great rolling deep lay in poetic descriptions have in common with a sea captain's daughter, wild to return to a world of ships and storms? Other things also troubled her and she took them to Ruth. The older woman had become a substitute mother, more so even than kindly Mrs. Grayson.

"Sometimes I feel Byron has made a god of Lord Byron," she told her friend one evening when the elder Graysons had gone out. The children slept in their rooms and the guests who had grown to be part of the family enjoyed a cheery fire in the sitting room. Its warm coziness offered a sense of relaxation lacking in the more formal parlor with its starched crocheted antimacassars and horsehair furniture.

"That happens." Ruth's hands stilled on the sweater she was knitting for Gretchen. "There is a great deal of modernism and letdown of standards even in the churches, Inga. Do you know where the professor stands on things of the Spirit?" She hesitated, then timidly added, "Even though he's been coming to church, I sometimes wonder—" She broke off as if afraid of offending.

"So do I," Inga admitted, blue eyes filled with uncertainty. "Some of the writers Byron admires most are those Father taught me were godless." She sighed, wishing for the joy she'd known that first night Byron took her to the reading circle. The last few times she attended, she had felt uncomfortable with the trend of skepticism that surfaced.

"I wish Father would come," she passionately cried, keeping her voice low so she wouldn't disturb the children. "I need to look at Byron through Father's eyes, not with my own. I've always been able to recognize wrong when I hear it. Some of the comments in class and at the reading circle sound innocent—but they make me wonder if they aren't insidiously designed to pull people away from God." She stared into the fire. "They teach the most important thing on earth is to be in control of your own destiny. The Bible says in the third chapter of Proverbs that we are to acknowledge God and let Him direct our lives. I know it's healthy to question, but a lot of my classmates aren't well enough acquainted with scripture to know if they're being led astray. Sometimes I even wonder if I am."

A little white line formed around her mouth. "I've been neglecting my Bible reading lately. No more. I intend to study harder than ever. I have the feeling I may need it in the next few months."

"You think Professor Irving is deliberately sowing seeds of atheism?"

"I don't know for sure, but I'm terribly afraid that's what is happening." Suddenly she realized how strongly she believed that very thing. A desire to confide surged through her and spilled out. "We were discussing the agnostic Thomas Huxley today. Byron said Huxley should be applauded for having the courage to point out that the existence of God or a spiritual world cannot be proved."

Anger and disappointment flowed through her. "I raised my hand to protest. I'm sure he saw it but he just kept on talking. Class ended and Byron was perfectly charming when I told him I didn't agree. He looked humble and said he hoped I'd always trust him enough to let me know how I felt." She fell silent, more discouraged and disturbed than she cared to admit. "I wonder if anyone would have listened if I had been given the chance to speak? Sometimes I think Byron has hypnotized the entire class." The last words came in a whisper. "I find myself thinking what he says is plausible. It's so hard to know what to do. I'm so much younger— I feel inadequate to stand up against learned men."

"My dear girl, you must not allow anyone to control your thinking except our Lord." Ruth took Inga's hands in her own. "Go to your heavenly Father. Remember James's instruction to us in his first chapter? When we lack wisdom, we're to ask in faith, without wavering. For he that wavereth is like a wave of the sea driven with the wind and tossed."

Inga closed her eyes, remembering tempests aboard the *Norseman*, the howling winds, groaning timbers, and tossing ship. "How well I know, Ruth. That's the way I am. This is worse than any storm I've ever known. Oh, if Father were only here!"

The teacher's voice gentled. "Inga, if this is truly how you feel, it is time for you to examine your heart. You must learn if Professor Irving has laid claim to that which you have consecrated to God." She slipped from her chair and knelt beside the distraught girl. Head bowed, she said nothing and after a time stood and left the room. Yet she left behind a wake of peace born from understanding and lack of condemnation. It gave Inga the courage to walk upstairs, take out her Bible, and seek God's will instead of her own.

December daylight found her still awake but calm. The stranglehold the visiting professor had begun to have on Inga's heart no longer existed. In the murky gray dawn she recognized it for what it had been: the excitement of being singled out and elevated above Byron's rank of admirers, combined with respect for his rich education in the classics. Love? Nay. A schoolgirl crush on a man who loved poetry and sought to be like his idols.

Inga's heart raced. How would she greet him, knowing the change in herself? "God," she prayed before leaving her room. "Give me strength for this day."

Hours later she stumbled home, gray-faced with fatigue and humiliation but sustained by her morning prayer. Professor Irving had not come to class. Rumors did, followed by the shocking truth. The president of the university had just learned Byron's credentials were nothing more than a clever forgery, product of an imaginative, unscrupulous mind. He immediately dismissed the bogus professor.

"I guess Irving fooled me and all of us." Fred, who continued to admire Inga long after the canoe race, sent a stormy stare around the classroom. Inga sensed he was warning anyone who dared speak. No one did. Her classmates deliberately changed the subject to plans for the upcoming holidays. Several reminded Inga of parties, the church banquet, Christmas services. Their loyal support helped her as nothing else could. So did the spirit of relief that fell over her like a blanket and got her through the day.

That night after Gretchen and young Tommy went to bed, Inga told the elder Graysons and Ruth what happened. "No wonder I felt something was wrong without knowing what or why. Suppose I'd actually been in love with him?" Cold shivers trotted up and down her spine at the thought. "One thing." She grew pensive and her blue eyes darkened. "It will be a long time before I let myself care about another man."

The Graysons exchanged wise glances and chuckled. Ruth warned, "Don't make rash promises, Inga. You never know what's on the next page of your life story." She shrewdly added, "Be glad it's your pride that's hurt, not your heart."

"I am," Inga fervently replied. A wide smile grew on her lips. "I'll wager dented pride heals a lot quicker than a broken heart!" Her merry laugh showed she had escaped far more lightly than expected and her friends rejoiced.

⁂

By the time January came and classes resumed, Professor Irving had all but been forgotten. A middle-aged professor with six children took his place. He concentrated on writers who did not question the Almighty's existence, and Inga sighed with relief. Yet aware now of how easily one could be swayed away by false doctrines, she continued to study her Bible daily.

Graduation loomed just a few short months away. Students—especially the seniors—studied early and late. Inga turned in several original and well-researched papers. One came to the president's desk. He called her in, gallantly seated her so she could see Mt. Rainier out a shining window, then took his place in a massive chair behind a cluttered desk and beamed at her.

"Miss Nansen, I have the honor to tell you I've spoken with others and am pleased to offer you an opportunity to do graduate work here at the university."

Inga felt herself pale. "I—I won't be in Seattle after graduation," she faltered.

"Why, Miss Nansen! You certainly won't turn down an opportunity to develop your writing skills, will you? With further training you could become part of our staff." He held up her theme and beamed again. "This is brilliant work. If it's a matter of finances, you need not worry. You're being given a full scholarship."

Pride throbbed in her heart and she felt mist rise to her eyes. "I cannot stay, sir. Not for all the scholarships in the world."

His mouth dropped open. She saw how flabbergasted he was to have anyone turn down such a ripe plum. "Are you getting married?" he bluntly asked. Suspicion showed in his eyes. "Miss Nansen, surely you haven't kept in touch with that bounder Irving!" Disapproval dripped from every word.

Inga felt her face redden, then the absurdity of it set off her sense of humor. Her bell-like laugh chimed. She saw his relief even before she said, "Hardly! There was nothing between us except friendship." How glad she was to be able to look clearly and honestly into the concerned president's face. Anticipation curled Inga's lips into a smile. "Father is coming for me. I'll be sailing with him on the *Flower of Alaska*. I just told him about completing my course a year early and he is ecstatic." She leaned forward, eyes glowing with pent-up emotions from almost three years. "He wanted me to have knowledge, so I came. But now I'm ready to go back to the sea."

Her simplicity obviously jolted the president. After a long, searching look he quietly asked, "Have you gained what your father hoped?"

Inga's heart beat faster. "May I speak frankly?"

"Of course." He placed his elbows on the desk, clasped his hands, and leaned his chin against them.

"I have gained much knowledge from my professors." She chose her words carefully. "Even Professor Irving, who turned out to be false, added to that store. The true wisdom I've received has come from another source."

"And that is—?"

"The Bible. It's the greatest book ever written and the only one that can truly prepare us to meet and face life." Inga's gaze never wavered. There! She'd said it, the message she longed to speak to her classmates that fateful day when she was denied the opportunity. She felt blood race into her face. A pulse pounded in her temple. What would this revered scholar say?

The president rose so quickly his chair swiveled back and crashed into the wall behind. He strode around his desk. Inga quailed. The next moment his hand shot out and engulfed hers. "Congratulations, Miss Nansen. If you had learned nothing else while attending the University of Washington— and I know you have—it has been worth your time and our efforts."

She smiled in relief, unable to speak.

The president dropped her hand, righted his chair, and sat down again. "I am curious. How do you plan to use your education on a boat?"

"Ship," she automatically corrected, then blushed at her

temerity. She quickly ticked off on her fingers. "I have enough knowledge to teach others basic reading, writing, arithmetic skills. My studies in history and geography and literature will one day enrich my children's lives." She blushed again but went on. "I took courses in first aid and added to the knowledge Father had taught me. In an emergency I can give temporary aid or do home nursing."

"Yes, indeed. I remember how you saved the child last summer."

Inga shook her head, with its sunny hair plaited in the old way. "No, sir. God saved the child. I could not have done it without His help."

"Be that as it may, if you hadn't been there, the little boy would have drowned." The president fished for a handkerchief and loudly blew his nose. For the second time he stood and strode to her chair. Inga rose.

"I am going to do an unprecedented thing," the keen-eyed man told her. "Miss Nansen, I retract all offers of a scholarship. Not because I find you unworthy. Nay. The University of Washington is proud to claim you as one of its own." He half turned and looked at the majestic mountain that dominated the Seattle skyline from its position miles away.

"I am also going to tell you something only God and my wife know. If it were not for the sense of responsibility I feel to my staff and students, I would leave the city. I cannot— yet. I've been put in this position for a reason. Until I know I've fulfilled it, I must stay, even when I long for hills and valleys, sea and shore. Someday I hope to follow my heart, as you are doing." Wistfulness showed in his eyes when he swung back toward Inga. "Godspeed, child. I wish all those who walk these halls of learning were as clear-eyed and faithful to their Creator as you are." He shook hands with her and ushered her to the heavy door. It closed behind her on well-oiled hinges, shutting him in with his duties, releasing her to a long-awaited renewal of the life she loved.

Inga stumbled from the president's office in a blur of tears. She felt the same way as when she discovered Ruth Perkins's unplumbed depths, and she wondered, if someday duty warred with her desire for freedom, would she be as faithful and true as the man who set aside his wishes to serve for the sake of others?

The warmth of the president's blessing sank deep into Inga's soul. A flash of insight much like the elusive green flash sometimes seen when the sun dropped behind the ocean's horizon whispered, *Graduation is several weeks away but this is your real commencement.*

❧

Inga carried the memory of the conversation as a talisman. She studied even harder, searched her Bible even more diligently. Days hurried into weeks. Weeks scurried into months. Never had Seattle been lovelier. A sense of urgency possessed Inga's soul, the feeling she must complete every task and leave nothing undone when she sailed. She spent hours with Ruth and cordially invited her to sail on the *Flower of Alaska.* The memory of how she had once inveigled the teacher aboard so she could see a certain picture brought a rueful smile to her lips. Then she had been afraid of Miss Perkins getting hurt. Now she hoped with all her heart the older woman would one day accept the invitation.

Inga brought nosegays to Mrs. Grayson, books she knew he would like to Mr. Grayson. She cherished each storytelling time with Gretchen and Tommy, grown so much since she first came.

"You aren't going away forever and ever, are you?"

Gretchen demanded one evening from Inga's bed where she and Tommy sat watching Inga stashing winter clothing in her big sea chest.

"No. I'll come back and visit you when I can." She straightened and smiled, knowing how hard it would be to leave the little girl and her brother. Would she one day have children as adorable as these? The question brought a flutter to her heart and she fervently hoped it would come to pass.

"Why are you going?" Tommy wanted to know. He squirmed until his sister told him to sit still, then plaintively added, "Don't you love us never no more?"

"Of course I do." Inga frantically searched for the right words. "Tommy, can you imagine how you or Gretchen would feel if you could only see your daddy now and then? Think how lonesome he would be. I miss my father so much." Tears just below the surface gushed like a waterspout.

"Don't cry, Inga!" Gretchen showed early signs of becoming the same kind of loving woman as her mother. Now she ran to her idol. "Of course you have to go with your father. He's coming soon, isn't he? You won't forget us never no more?"

"Never no more," Tommy echoed past the finger in his mouth.

"I won't forget you never no more," Inga solemnly and ungrammatically promised. "Father will be here for graduation." She felt a drop spill and roll but turned away so the children wouldn't see it. "It's been so long. He got held up before. I hope nothing happens to delay him this time."

Alas for Inga's wishes. She received a telegram just hours before time for the exercises. The *Flower of Alaska* had been slightly damaged in a storm. Repairs in Vancouver took longer than expected. By the time Lars realized he couldn't sail to Seattle, he was too late to get there by another means. *"I will be there in spirit,"* the telegram read. *"Think of it as just a squall. We have a thousand sunrises coming."*

"It's not as if you're without family," Ruth cheered. "Sally and Dick are coming. The Graysons and I will be there in our Sunday best." She smiled at the disappointed girl. "I know it isn't the same, but what is one ceremony compared with the days and nights you and your father will share?"

The practical advice worked. Inga proudly stepped forward and accepted her diploma and honors, knowing at that very moment her father stood looking south, rejoicing that their self-imposed separation was all but over.

Ten days later the fully restored *Flower of Alaska* sailed into the Seattle harbor. Not trusting herself to first see her father on the ship, Inga had sent a wire asking him to meet her at a restaurant they frequently patronized on his visits. She dressed with unusual care and mischievously asked Ruth to do her hair in the new way. "I want him to see me as a fine lady, then I'll go back to being his Inga," she explained.

On the afternoon of their reunion, Inga reached the restaurant early. Lars stood waiting with open arms. Ignoring the curious stares of other patrons, Inga threw her fine manners to the wind, raced toward him, and called, "Huff and puff all you like, Captain. Your First Mate has served her time. I'm sailing with you on the *Flower of Alaska* if I have to stow away!"

"Bully for you," a deep, amused voice behind her approved.

Face still aglow with fun, Inga whipped around to find a stranger gazing at her with laughing blue eyes only a shade less brilliant than her own.

eight

Arthur Baldwin had paid little heed to the vastness of Canada and Alaska Territory until he learned Bern Clifton might dwell somewhere within their confines. After Dr. Aldrich stepped forward and volunteered to go to the Hollow, Arthur studied everything he could find about the north country. Thousands of miles stretched silent, holding secret the whereabouts of the man he had loved and wronged. Arthur's spirits sank. Looking for someone in the mostly uninhabited land equaled the preposterous task of seeking one snowflake in a howling blizzard.

Benjamin Clifton pleaded with the young doctor to abide with him during the winter months. "You cannot embark on your journey now with any hope of success," he flatly stated. "Late spring and early summer hold the only key able to unlock a place covered with snow and ice."

Arthur recognized the validity of the older man's arguments, even though hot blood poured through his veins in a fury of eagerness to leave Philadelphia. He continued working at whatever he could find and stayed strictly away from his ancestral mansion. Neither did Julia Langley trouble Arthur.

"I didn't expect her to," he wryly told Benjamin. "I'm sure Mother or Father have told Julia I am beyond the pale and written out of their will."

"If such keeps her from standing by you then she does not care," Benjamin observed.

Arthur leaned back in his comfortable chair and laughed aloud. The sound rang in the quiet, firelit room and brought a smile to the listener's face. "She never did. Julia Langley will always care for herself and tolerate others, especially those with bright futures. The one thing I am glad of in this whole horrible mess is that Bern—and I—both escaped marrying her."

"It is a blessing. Arthur, you realize the trail you must take to find my son will be hard and long." Benjamin fit the tips of his fingers together and leaned forward. "I don't believe either of us can have any idea of how rugged the country, how high the mountains you cross will be." He mused, then added, "If ever you are tempted to turn back, I will understand."

"I shall never turn back!" Arthur sprang to his feet and paced the spotless but worn carpet. "Once life, hope, and dreams burned inside your son like a torch. I extinguished the flame. I know now nothing or no one can relight it except God. I may be the only person who can show Bern the way back. Nay, the way up." A look of wonder crossed Arthur's face. Some of the old sweetness crept into his wistful blue eyes. "If Jesus could go to the cross for me, surely I can face Canada and Alaska for Bern."

Week after week, month after month, the two who loved and had wronged Bernard Clifton made their plans. Arthur spent every free moment adding to the magnificent store of strength he had accumulated while in North Carolina. He ran morning and night, rejoicing when a mile turned to two, then three. He learned a long, steady stride actually covered more territory than short bursts of speed followed by rest. He increased his speed until even the prowess that had made him one of the finest runners on track and field paled by comparison.

With the first crocus, his desire to be off intensified. Only Benjamin's restraint held him back. "Spring comes far earlier to Philadelphia than where you will be going," he reminded. "Give it a little more time, son."

Arthur never failed to thrill at the word *son*. It always brought a pang. If only he and his father could be close! A few days before he left the city, he attempted to see his family. A sober, fearful butler shook his head and closed the door in Arthur's face. The doctor's last sight of the house that had never earned the title *home* was of closed shutters, closed hearts and minds. He sadly penned a note and posted it the afternoon before he left. In it he repeated what he had told Arthur Baldwin, Senior. He would love and pray for his parents always.

The next morning he boarded the train destined to carry him on his first lap of what he recognized might be a journey of years. On the step, he surveyed the small crowd gathered at the station, hoping beyond hope to see his father's face. A pang went through him and he regretted bidding Benjamin good-bye at home. No friendly face stood out in the crowd. No hand waved to him. Dr. Arthur Baldwin, once the pride of the house of Baldwin, left as he had come back from North Carolina, without fanfare, without farewell.

He set his lips in the straight line Donald MacDonald knew so well and turned his face north and west. Somewhere in the thousands of empty miles, there must be a clue to lead him to his quarry. A thrill went through Arthur. What did it matter that in all of Philadelphia only one man believed in him, prayed for him? Had not God promised in the Gospel of John, chapter fourteen, never to leave those who served Him? His abiding Spirit would go with His forgiven child into whatever lay ahead.

ঌ

Weeks later Arthur reached the place where Bern started his terse, long-ago message to his father. Too much time and too many wanderers had tramped through. No one remembered Bern.

"That ain't to say he warn't here," a trading post owner frankly admitted from beneath peaked eyebrows. "Sonny, in this country, we ain't much on askin' questions. A man's business is his own. If he states it, well and good. If not. . ." His significant shrug finished the sentence. It also became the usual answer, along with a suspicious, "What's he wanted for?"

Arthur learned to escape when those he questioned turned the tables and grew inquisitive.

Weeks passed. Arthur lost track of how many trails he'd trod in response to faint clues that faded faster than footprints on solid rock. North, south, east, and west he traveled, thrilling to the scope and breadth of the country. Across Canada. Into Alaska Territory, called "Seward's Folly" and "Seward's Ice Box" after the far-sighted Secretary of State who had insisted the United States purchase it from Russia at about two cents an acre.

Now and then someone recollected seeing or hearing of someone who might have been Bern. Yet at the end of two years, a disheartened and gaunt Dr. Noble, as he still ironically called himself, felt no nearer his journey's end than when he left Philadelphia.

He'd holed into a miserable excuse of a town the first winter and almost gone mad until he met up with a trapper who needed help. Arthur smiled to himself. His fine surgeon's hands grew expert at skinning the catch and stretching fine pelts but the work kept him outdoors and hardened his body even more.

The next winter he spent in Vancouver. He found it even worse, except there he found a place working in a hospital. He told the hospital superintendent he had left the East for personal reasons, asked for a chance to show his skills, and won the admiration of the entire staff. He also eagerly questioned all under his care who knew anything about the north country, but to no avail.

When the Klondike Gold Rush began, Arthur considered heading there. On second thought he shook his head—and made a fatal error in judgment. "Bern wouldn't be caught dead in such a place," he decided, failing to take into account possible changes in his friend's standards.

Time became meaningless. Arthur left the Vancouver hospital armed with glowing recommendations that would get him a job in any hospital that needed a fine surgeon. Again he faced chasms and peaks, tundra and muskeg. He trod on ground so frozen it seemed impossible the hottest summer sun could melt it. He watched the same ground yield berries, fruits, vegetables, and flowers that made him gasp at their size. More and more he turned his back on Canada and concentrated on Alaska Territory. The months and years took their toll. A few streaks of silver gleamed in his sunny yellow hair. Lines formed at the corner of his searching blue eyes, born of straining to look long distances and marveling at the aurora borealis.

His heart swelled within him. Out of evil, good had come. Suppose he had never known this land. The thought cut off his breath. Never to have known the exaltation of standing in a high mountain pass with even taller peaks in the distance? Never to run behind a dogsled in subzero weather so cold it froze his breath on the woolen scarf over nose and mouth? Or thrill to the knowledge only the hand of God could be responsible for the churning rivers, the animals who inhabited field and forest?

How far away Philadelphia seemed. At times, Arthur felt he had stepped from one lifetime into another. Alaska Territory offered contrasts so great he had trouble comprehending them. Incomparable beauty, incredible cruelty. It allowed for no mistakes, especially in winter. Twice Arthur had been caught out at the beginning of a blizzard. In both instances he found shelter—once in a hut fetid with smoke and unwashed humanity, the other by stumbling onto a party of travelers who made room for him in an already-crowded tent. He repaid the latter by delivering a baby who saw no reason to delay his coming until his parents reached a distant village. Arthur thanked God for shelter from storm and for the opportunity to serve.

What stories he and Bern could share if only he could find his old friend! Arthur's longing deepened, yet vague fears haunted him. Bern might have gone elsewhere to escape the harsh winters, the never-ending battle for survival in the last frontier. Perhaps his friend lay in an unmarked grave somewhere in the endless land. At this point in his thinking, Arthur clamped down hard. Surely God would not let Bern die in bitterness against father and friend. He bowed his head and prayed as he had done so often, asking God to direct him.

Another winter melted into spring, then summer. Word of a white man and his lovely daughter who lived and worked among an isolated Indian tribe sang in the rushing streams, whispering aspens, and cottonwoods. It piqued Arthur's curiosity. "Who and where are they?" he asked Jean Langlois, a French Canadian *coureur de bois* (woods runner) who had been mauled by a bear near Fairbanks, where Dr. Noble presently worked. Wilderness forays required more than came to him quarterly and required him to supplement his income in order to outfit himself.

The Frenchman's pain-twisted face brightened and he stoically endured the doctor's cleansing of his wounds. "*M'sieu*, they are angels! I have not seen but I swear by what is holy, the Great Father Himself sent them to this cursed land."

Arthur had long grown used to those who berated the country but would live no other place. He patiently waited for the musical voice to continue, knowing the man could not be hurried.

"Nicolai Anton and his daughter An-a-sta-sia are beloved by all. They make a home in the wilderness with their trading post. Did they not take in my own brother and care for him as if he were their own when he stumbled into Tarnigan ill with the fever?" Jean's dark eyes and white teeth glistened.

"Tarnigan?" Arthur liked the sound of it on his tongue.

"*Oui, M'sieu* Noble. Tarnigan, she sit in the shadow of the Endicott Mountains, halfway between here and Pt. Barrow on the Arctic Ocean." The injured man pointed north. "All who know say even the birds in the bush sing praises all day long. An-a-sta-sia means resurrection, of springtime." He quickly crossed himself. "Nicolai calls his daughter Little Flower. Others call her Sasha."

"Have they been in Tarnigan long?"

Jean spread his arms wide. "Ever since they built *Nika Illahee* which means 'my dear homeland.'" His smile gleamed again. "One day I will go there."

"To win Sasha?" Arthur idly asked, fingers busy wrapping layers of gauze.

"*M'sieu!*" Anger stiffened Jean's body. "The blood of the

great Alexander Baranof flows in her veins, as well as that of a French mother and an Indian princess ancestor. *Little Flower* is not for a poor runner of the woods. Besides, I have my Fanchon." His eyes glittered. "Neither is An-a-sta-sia's name to be taken lightly. By anyone." His dark gaze didn't waver by the fraction of an inch.

"I meant no disrespect," Arthur penitently told his patient. "Forgive me."

Suspicion died. A bright smile bloomed again. "Ah. Once you see An-a-sta-sia you will understand." He flung a bandaged hand over his heart. "Any man who knows her would gladly give his life to save her honor."

Arthur marveled at the words. An errant thought crossed his mind. How many men would die for Julia Langley's honor? The desire to meet the remarkable Sasha Anton and her father stirred within him.

"She is not yet twenty and lovely," Jean rattled on. "I think she will marry one Ivan Romanov, who manages the trading post for Nicolai." The corners of his mouth turned down. "He is not worthy of her." With another lightning shift of mood he cheered up. "My brother says the beautiful An-a-sta-sia should marry on Hoots-Noo."

"Who is he, a native?" Arthur asked, not because he particularly cared but to keep Langlois talking. Something in the engaging Frenchman's voice intrigued the doctor.

Jean's eyes opened wide and he delivered a blow straight to Arthur's soul. "Oh, no, *M'sieu* Noble. Hoots-Noo, 'heart of a grizzly,' is a man of medicine, like you. No one knows from where he came, but the people of the far country say he brings healing to them." Jean warmed to the subject. "He goes wherever he is needed. I think he might be a good mate for the blessed An-a-sta-sia."

Arthur's hands mechanically finished his task. He swallowed hard. "What is the doctor's real name?" Blood pounded in his temples and he held his breath.

Jean shrugged, the essence of Gallic insouciance. "My brother did not say. Perhaps he does not know. Hoots-Noo is a good name. To have the heart of a grizzly is a great thing. Does it matter what else he is called?"

The doctor didn't answer. He turned away and fumbled with his instruments until he could get himself under control. Yet even as he ordered Jean to stay put for a day so he could check on him before he left Fairbanks, Arthur wanted to leap for joy. For the first time since he left Philadelphia, he had a clue worth following. *Bernard*, "brave bear." *Hoots-Noo*, "heart of a grizzly." Could it be mere chance? Nay, Arthur's heart whispered. The arm of coincidence is long, but does not stretch so far.

Arthur tried to ignore the leaping expectation inside him. He could not leave Fairbanks until another inheritance payment came. He had also given his word to the physician he assisted he would stay at least six months. Not even to find out if this mysterious Hoots-Noo were indeed Bern Clifton could he break his promise. He longed to write to Benjamin and squelched the wish. How well he knew the anguish of false hopes raised then unrealized. Nay, he must wait, pray and dream.

Weakness overtook him. In spite of all his preparation, he realized he still didn't know how to approach Bern. Should he send a letter? Jean Langlois had expressed appreciation for the patching job, as he called it, and sworn undying loyalty. He could be trusted to carry a message.

Arthur shook his head. He could not take the chance of having the message burned if hatred still flared high. "God, if I could only see him, learn how he feels, without his know-ing me." The idea took hold. Was there a way to disguise himself so completely Bern would not recognize him?

Again he shook his head. Bern knew him too well. Hands, face, body. Why, even his voice would betray him. Arthur reluctantly laid aside the idea.

Time had crawled at a snail's pace before. Now Arthur felt it went backward. He remained conscientious to his work but once he completed it for the day, his blue gaze stretched north and west. Despite everything he did to discourage it, hope ran through him like a northern river in flood when the ice goes out. A month. Two. Another month and another. Soon Arthur would be free, but he still didn't know how to approach Bern, if it turned out he and Hoots-Noo were the same man. The cheerful Jean had healed and gone back to his Fanchon. No more word came of Tarnigan or its inhabitants.

At last Arthur finished his stint in Fairbanks and rejoiced. Now he could trek to Tarnigan. It was not to be. That very day Jean Langlois returned, accompanied by a thin-faced girl whose great dark eyes shone with trust. "*M'sieu*, my Fanchon is not well. Will you help her?" Childlike faith showed in his face.

Arthur did a lightning examination. "She needs surgery. She's not in danger right now but she will be soon. Jean, I don't have the proper equipment here." He looked the French-man straight in the eye. "It's a long way to Vancouver but we have to go, before she worsens."

"When do we start?"

Arthur's hand clasped the other's. "Tomorrow morning."

He never knew how they accomplished the journey, only that God and the wilderness grapevine opened a way. The silent forests spewed out strong men who willingly aided them in their race for life at every turn. Fanchon's refusal to give up spurred them on. Arthur laid aside his longing for Tarnigan and concentrated on the present situation. They fought and won. Once they reached Vancouver and allowed Fanchon to rest for a few days, a masked, gowned doctor picked up a shining scalpel and confidently made the first incision. Hours later he discarded stained, sweaty garments, raced to the waiting room, and embraced Jean.

"She will live to have many children and grandchildren, God willing," he choked out through the gladness that filled him.

Jean said nothing, but his look of gratitude started a freshet in the surgeon's eyes until the slim woods runner blurred before him.

nine

Fanchon's magnificent strength served her well. Bright color returned to her sallow cheeks, a sparkle to the eyes that held adoration for her husband and reverence for her doctor. Arthur had never cared for a better patient. She healed rapidly and a few weeks later, he bid her and Jean farewell.

Once the crisis passed, the French Canadian came to Arthur, face furrowed with worry. "*M'sieu*, the bills—they are many." A white smile flashed like breakers on a dark reef and he snapped his fingers. "They are nothing compared with the life of my Fanchon." The smile faded. "We have little money but we can pay in the spring. All winter Jean Langlois and his Fanchon will trap animals for their skins. Will the good hospital wait so long?"

"It's already been taken care of," Arthur told him.

Jean's eyes opened wide in astonishment. "How is such a thing possible?"

Arthur chose his words carefully. "In some instances hospitals waive the fees. My fellow physicians are impressed by your getting Fanchon here under such conditions. You are to pay nothing." *I didn't say Fanchon's hospital fees had been waived,* he told his conscience. *If Jean knew it took all my quarterly stipend to pay them, he would never accept.*

Jean cocked his dark head to one side. His gaze bored into Arthur's. "You say nothing of your own fee, my friend."

Arthur's hand shot out and a spontaneous smile sprang to his face. "Jean, God has given me skills. Why should I not use them for my friends?" He sensed a growing undercur-

102

rent of protest in the proud man before him. "Would you not take me in and care for me, if you found me helpless outside your door? Perhaps one day I will have need of your friendship and your knowledge of the wild."

"*Oui.*" Jean's woods-trained hand gripped Arthur's. A beautiful light came to his glistening eyes. "*M'sieu,* my Fanchon and I will name our first son for you. He shall be called Noble Langlois."

Arthur had to turn away from the deep emotion in Jean's rich voice. Jean's eyes would flash with scorn if he knew how ignoble the doctor before him had been. The law of the north that ruled the *coureur de bois* required a man to die before betraying a friend. Breaking that law was second only to the law of the cache. Robbing another of carefully hoarded food meant death. Betrayal brought inner death. Arthur shivered. Until he could face Bern Clifton, something in his own heart also remained dead.

Jean and Fanchon left a few weeks later. They would work their way north, sure of a welcome wherever a lonely cabin huddled in the wilderness. Summer had gone; autumn lay warm and smiling over the land. The travelers could still reach their home beyond Fairbanks long before winter's heavy hand descended.

Arthur bid the slim woods runner and his lovely Fanchon farewell. A pang went through him. Would he ever be companioned by a laughing wife who looked into his face and cared little who saw her love for her mate? He tried to fit Julia into the picture and failed miserably. His mouth twitched at the thought of her sleeping under the stars and eating camp food.

Amusement died. What should he do now? The hospital had a place for him but the idea of wintering in Vancouver held little attraction. Should he have gone trapping with Jean? He considered going after his friends but rejected the idea. Jean had Fanchon and needed no other helper. The furs they accumulated would give them a start on providing a home for young Noble when he arrived sometime in the future.

"I have to work," Arthur muttered. "God, where do You want me? I can't go to Tarnigan until I earn outfitting money and the next quarter's draft comes. By that time, mountains, streams, and valleys will be locked tight with snow and ice." He sighed. "Should I just stay here?"

No answer came to his troubled mind so Arthur wisely determined to simply remain at the Vancouver hospital until something turned up. If it did not, he would continue where he was.

A week passed. Another. One dreary afternoon rain sluiced down the window of the boarding house where Arthur sprawled in an uncomfortable chair. He scanned the newspaper advertisements, as he did with each new edition. Half asleep from boredom and fatigue, he jerked erect when his gaze reached a small advertisement.

HELP WANTED:
Doctor for SS *Flower of Alaska*
Top wages to right man. Contact
Captain L. Nansen, Klondike Hotel.
Ship sails end of this week.

Wings of excitement beat in Arthur's brain. His weariness and boredom changed to anticipation. Visions of tossing seas and far vistas danced in the air before him. "God, is this Your answer?" He laughed aloud and reread the ad. "Wonder what Captain Lars Nansen considers top wages?

He's mighty particular, saying that about the right man."

An hour later, encased in a dripping oilskin, Arthur stepped onto the porch of a modest rooming house and into a new chapter of his life. He shrugged out of his wet coat and left it on the porch. Tall, straight, and outwardly calm, he walked inside, hoping Captain Nansen wouldn't hear his thundering heartbeat.

Nansen turned out much as Arthur expected—a true son of Scandinavia. The two men shook hands, taking stock of one another before either spoke.

Arthur liked what he saw. This craggy captain had humor as well as far-sightedness in his weathered face. A gleam in the sea-blue eyes showed the extent of the sea captain's interest. It gave Arthur the courage to bluntly say, "I'd like to sail with you, Captain Nansen, if we can come to terms." He described his training and experience.

Frank approval showed in the other's eyes and hearty, "So you've worked under primitive conditions. Ever performed surgery at sea in the midst of a raging gale?"

"No, but if a life needs saving, I'm game to try," Arthur retorted.

Lars gave a bellow of laughter. A heavy hand fell to the doctor's shoulder. "You're hired." He named a princely sum. "Just one thing. I need your word you will stay with the *Flower of Alaska* at least a year."

A year? Arthur felt keenly disappointed. By that time, Bern might be anywhere. There was no guarantee he would stay in Tarnigan that long. On the other hand, Hoots-Noo might turn out to be some other white doctor and Arthur would have sacrificed adventure and an interesting job for nothing.

"Is the pay not enough for you?" Nansen demanded

scornfully.

"It's more than fair and I'd love to take the job." Arthur spread his fine, surgeon's hands wide. "It's just that I can't promise to stay a year. I have personal business that must not be delayed longer than late spring or early summer when the northern snows melt."

"So pressing you would turn me down." The keen gaze never left Arthur's troubled face.

"I have no choice." Arthur took a long, deep breath. "I wronged someone long ago. Now I have a lead to his whereabouts." He desperately added, "I've repented a hundredfold. I am forgiven—by God. Now I must make what restitution I can and learn to forgive myself." Why had he blurted out his innermost feelings? What cared this stranger for the restlessness that drove him as the winds drove the *Flower of Alaska*? Arthur continued to gaze straight into the captain's face; he felt Lars Nansen sensed far more than what had been spoken.

At last Lars said, "Sail with me, son, until the time comes you must go. A man must follow his proddings." The gruff words touched Arthur's soul and became part of him.

ર

Three days later Arthur, still under the name of Dr. Noble, boarded the *Flower of Alaska* and steamed out of Vancouver. He couldn't say why he quixotically clung to his alias. Perhaps the passing years had ingrained it into him. Or the desire to make good before his father could trace him had something to do with it. In any case, he signed on as Dr. Noble.

His Spartan quarters suited him well. So did Captain Lars, by turn both taciturn and loquacious. Arthur learned to know and love the sea, the sky, the illimitable expanses that rolled on forever. He enjoyed contact with the passengers who had become an important part of the steamship's cargo. The lure of Alaskan gold kept a steady stream of humanity turned northward.

Lars proved a satisfying companion. He proudly showed his new doctor the picture of Inga he carried over his heart. "It does her no justice," he said deprecatingly.

Arthur peered at the sweet face. "She is lovely." Yet something in his voice kept the captain from saying more. Arthur couldn't explain how the picture brought back memories of blonde Julia, who had created havoc. He looked at the picture a second time and classified Inga Nansen as far above Julia. The innocence in eyes he knew would be blue as her father's contrasted sharply with another pair of eyes that meltingly promised, then grew hard with greed.

Lars never tired of sharing with his eager doctor-pupil the information he had gathered over many years. The first time they steamed up the Inside Passage he admitted, "I never tire of it. Probably because for many years I sailed out of sight of land. This waterway's never far from land, the coast on one side, forested islands on the other most of the way." He expertly guided his ship through crouching fog and the multitude of sharp turns that made steering difficult.

"How can you do it?" Arthur marveled.

"Son, I know the waterway well and keep my *Flower* in the middle by listening to the echo of the ship's whistle." His laugh boomed out.

When they came to Ketchikan, he said, "It's known as Alaska's Gateway or First City. It served as a supply base and port for miners during the gold rush. I had men who possessed little more than the clothing they wore sleeping on the deck." He wagged his silver-streaked blond head.

"Many lost their lives from greed. Better if they'd remained with their fishing boats."

Arthur eyed the sprawling village through which the hordes had gone on their way to the Klondike. Unprepossessing, it yet held a certain charm, and Arthur went ashore to explore the hamlet in its picturesque setting. He hadn't gone more than a few steps before a low moan from behind baled cargo stopped him. He rounded the stack. A ragged blanket covered a prone form.

Instantly professional, Arthur knelt, threw back the covering and gasped. Dull black eyes stared at him. Swollen, angry bruises and raised welts marred a brown-skinned face until it scarcely seemed human. One arm lay limp at an angle that proclaimed it broken. "Why'd I leave my bag on ship?" Arthur mumbled. "On the other hand, who knew I'd need it here?"

The injured man made no further sound. He neither struggled nor relaxed while Arthur carefully examined him. "Who are you?" the doctor demanded, fingers busy probing. "Who did this to you?" Long experience in Vancouver had shown him plenty of fight victims but none like this.

From the pallid, bleeding lips came a single word. "Strongheart."

"He's nothin' but a stinkin' Siwash," someone behind them sneered. "Don't waste yer time on sich."

Arthur rose and glared at the runty, squint-eyed man in fishy-smelling clothing who had come up. "He is a badly hurt human being. Stay with him while I go for my doctor's bag." He took a step, halted at the raucous laughter issuing from between tobacco-stained teeth.

"Me nurse an Injun?" An obscenity followed, then avarice replaced scorn in the faded eyes. "Course, fer consid'ration, I 'low I cud watch him fer a spell."

Arthur snatched a bill from his pocket and flung it down.

"Ain'tcha got gold?" the man whined.

"No." Arthur started off in a long stride, then whirled back. "If you have any ideas about leaving before I get back, forget them. If you aren't here, I'll hunt you down and beat the living daylights out of you!" Never had he threatened anyone, but he knew the harsh words were all this miserable excuse for a man would understand.

Fear shone naked in the wretch's face. "I reck'n I'll be here," he mumbled. "Jest don't 'xpect me to touch him."

"I wouldn't let you touch him for all the gold in the Mother Lode," Arthur snapped. He cast a glance at the Indian, met his impassive gaze and called, "I'll be back soon." The man merely closed his eyes, obviously weakened from loss of blood and lying exposed to the elements for who knew how long.

True to his uncertain word, the dubious nurse remained on duty until Arthur returned, accompanied by Lars. A second later, he shuffled off, loudly condemning "fool doctors an' sea cap'ns who didn't have brains enuf to let the stinkin' savage die."

"What are we going to do with him?" Arthur worried aloud. "If that fine specimen heading for the nearest saloon is representative of the good people of Ketchikan, the Indian will be a corpse before anyone raises a hand to help him."

Compassion shone in Lars's kindly, rugged face. "We'll take him with us, of course. I've never yet left anything hurt by the wayside."

Arthur administered a restorative and the Indian's eyes flickered open.

"Strongheart, Captain Nansen and I want to take you on board the *Flower of Alaska*. I can't properly set your arm here." He bound it to the man's side. "Can you walk if we help you?"

Strongheart nodded. Yet by the time they had him aboard the ship, great drops of sweat stood out on his puffy forehead and his lips closed until they looked like a seam in a sail. With the captain's help, Arthur anesthetized him just enough to set the arm properly, rejoicing over the clean break. They bathed Strongheart's body, emaciated to little more than bone and sinew, and clothed him in garments from Arthur's wardrobe.

"He's no ordinary Siwash," Lars observed. "There's a touch of something different from somewhere." He sighed. "The coming of the white man to Alaska has gone hard with the natives. They've been exploited and used. I'd say Strongheart may have some of the white strain in him, worse luck."

Arthur flinched and hoped the other didn't notice. The subject of mixed races brought a flood of memories he held in reserve until he could meet Bern again.

Good food, rest, and sea air worked wonders, as did Dr. Noble's prayers for the man whose life he had saved. Within a few days, Strongheart refused to stay in bed. He never told who attacked him, but dogged Arthur's footsteps. Lars explained that many tribes believed if a man saved someone's life, that person belonged to him. When Strongheart stood out of earshot, observing the Inside Passage with brooding eyes, Lars wisely added "Accept it, at least for now. Once he is well, he may want to go back among his people."

Arthur gradually learned more of his new friend. Strongheart, all the name he would give, did carry both Indian and white blood. He had been educated in a white man's school but found no place in that world. Neither did he feel at home with his tribe. He'd wandered where he pleased, never finding the acceptance his dark eyes showed he desperately hungered to receive. Strongheart spoke good English and his comprehension surprised Arthur. An idea grew in the doctor's head. Why not teach the Indian the rudiments of medicine? They'd be useful wherever he went once he left the *Flower of Alaska*. Arthur's lips twisted. In dire circumstances, even a prejudiced miner or trader would take help from an Indian rather than die for lack of medical attention. He approached Strongheart.

"Is this what Dr. Noble wishes me to do?" his patient asked.

"Only if you wish to learn," Arthur assured him. "Someday it may serve you well. In the meantime, there are cases right here on board where I need an extra pair of hands. Captain Nansen must guide the ship."

Never had Arthur worked with one quicker to learn, or as the days passed, more eager. Before long, the skilled surgeon knew when he wanted an instrument it would be ready before he asked. He also reaped a greater reward. In some obscure way, he felt himself atoning through teaching Strongheart.

Days, weeks, months passed. Captain Lars openly mourned the coming of spring and Arthur's need to leave him. Paradoxically, he also beamed with anticipation. "It's been too long since I saw my Inga," he told Arthur one night when the North Star shone behind them and countless constellations filled the navy velvet sky with wonder. Lars heaved a sigh. "Thank God it will be soon. She graduates with honors. You will attend the ceremonies with me."

Fate laughed in their faces. Less than an hour later, great black clouds scudded across the sky, blotting out the stars.

The worst storm Arthur had seen in his entire life blew up so quickly even experienced Captain Nansen was hard put to control the *Flower of Alaska*. Waves like monstrous sea beasts threatened to swallow the gallant ship and all aboard. Arthur ministered to passengers so sick they neither knew nor cared that the Indian Strongheart assisted.

Morning dawned in awful colors of cerise and angry yellow. The storm continued, damaging the ship. Not to the point of life endangerment, but necessitating the need to change their Seattle-bound course and get to Vancouver for repairs.

With each day, Lars grew more dispirited. He'd been told the vessel would be ready in plenty of time. The trouble proved to be far more serious than they'd thought. By then, no transportation would get them to Seattle in time for Inga's commencement. Arthur tried to cheer his friend. "What is a ceremony, after all? Even one where your daughter is honored? Thank God the hidden damage was discovered now. Suppose it had gone undetected? All of us, including your new first mate, could have drowned."

Lars's face cleared. "You are right." He sighed. "Arthur, I feel I am gaining a daughter but losing a son. Inga will sail north with us, but once we reach Alaska, you will depart. I pray one day you can come back."

"If God wills it."

"What about you?" The captain turned to the silent member of the trio.

"I will go with Dr. Noble," Stongheart said in his resonant voice.

☙

Ten days after Inga's graduation, the fully repaired *Flower of Alaska* steamed into Seattle. Arthur found himself strangely reluctant to meet the girl whose eyes had once shone with simple goodness. Long years had passed since the picture had been made. Lars' heart would break if the sweet face were changed, the trusting eyes clouded with doubt of God and His creation. True and noble men taught in universities, but so did those who looked to themselves for answers and planted their seeds of self-aggrandizement in those they led. Arthur found himself suspecting that Inga would not be the same girl her father remembered so lovingly.

ten

Dr. Arthur Baldwin and Captain Lars Nansen reached the restaurant Inga had named a full hour before the appointed time. Both shone with the spit and polish the occasion demanded. Not a wrinkle marred the captain's uniform or the dress suit the young doctor had purchased in Vancouver and had planned to wear to the commencement. The headwaiter showed them to a table in a quiet corner. Each time patrons entered, Lars's blue eyes anxiously scanned their faces.

"This is ridiculous," he muttered. He drummed his fingertips on the table and grinned until laugh wrinkles deepened. "Inga's always prompt but she won't be here—" He broke off and leaped to his feet.

Arthur involuntarily rose and stepped to one side at the look on his friend's face, unwilling to intrude in the first moment of greeting. A feeling of dread crept through him. Would Inga be all her picture promised?

He forced himself to look up. A vision of loveliness in sea-blue frilled with lace creamy as ocean foam stood in the doorway. A golden crown of hair held sparkling combs. Arthur felt keen disappointment. Where was the laughing girl in the photograph with her heavy braids and wide smile? He preferred her to the elegant young woman gazing around the room.

The next instant, Inga hurled herself toward them like a swell at sea. The closer she came the more Arthur revised his first impression. She was everything the photograph had shown. Nay, more. No man could look into Inga Nansen's face and fail to see her purity. Her expressive eyes showed she had known pain, yet unalloyed joy rang in her laughing voice when she flung herself into her father's great arms and challenged, "Huff and puff all you like, Captain. Your First Mate has served her time. I'm sailing with you on the *Flower of Alaska* if I have to stow away!"

"Bully for you," Arthur burst out in admiration and relief. Despite the exquisite frock and shining hair, a true daughter of the sea stood before him.

Inga turned and looked straight into his eyes, face aglow with fun. Not a bold look, but one of comradeship born of sharing a special moment. Arthur felt the same measuring he'd known when he met Lars in the Klondike Hotel months earlier. He wondered: why should the single glance of an unknown girl make him more alive than he had felt in years? He felt the same way he did each time the morning sun rose in splendor to herald a new day.

Lars gave them no time for introspection. His familiar laugh bellowed out. "A Swede keeps his word. Go you shall, even though my ship will never be the same with a fine lady like you aboard. Every man who sails with me will mutiny and oust me as captain so he can do your bidding." Pride underscored every word and he held her at arm's length. "Let's have a look at you."

Inga laughed, a merry trill that curled into Arthur's heart and warmed it like a fire in winter. "This is just for tonight," she confessed and sent Arthur a quick glance from beneath lashes that made half moons on her clear pink and white skin each time she looked down. She freed herself from her father's hold and pirouetted. "Aren't I splendid?" She abandoned her pose. "Father, you're forgetting your manners. Who is your companion?"

Lars roared again. "Who wouldn't be forgetting such things when his lone chick turns out to be a lady second only in beauty to her beloved mother?" He cleared his throat and gruffly said, "This is Doctor Noble, Inga. He's been ship doctor for some time now and knows all about you."

Arthur cringed. With an introduction like that, the girl would surely simper and say something inane or flirtatious.

She did neither. "That's nice. Then it won't take so long to get acquainted, will it?" Inga extended her hand and took his. No limp, ladylike shake, either, but a real grip that showed strength. Bemused, Arthur privately wondered if she represented a new type of womanhood. Inga Nansen certainly didn't fit into the slot of females he knew back East!

From robust chowder to flaky apple pie, Lars and Inga chattered with Arthur listening. A hundred different expressions chased across the girl's face, like rainbows reflecting on a glacier. Never had the widely traveled doctor met a more transparently honest person or one who fascinated him so completely. He sensed hidden, untouched depths in this daughter of the fjords. A pang of regret filled him. Except for the short time it took to sail north, he'd have little chance to get to know her better and he wanted to do so with every beat of his awakening heart. Although Inga little resembled Jean Langlois's Fanchon, Arthur would stake his life the same noble spirit dwelt in Inga that he'd sensed in the dark-eyed girl who loved and followed her mate. Inga would do likewise, no matter how hard the trail or where it led.

He fell into a daydream of completing his self-imposed task, then seeking Inga out. It rudely shattered when Lars jovially asked, "No man stole you away from me while I sailed, did they, daughter?"

She shook her head, but her natural color receded. "No." A second later, a steadfast look returned to her face. It told Arthur she'd weathered whatever storms clouded her life and had kept on course.

"There must be something wrong with the men of Seattle, eh, Noble?"

Jolted from his preoccupation by the fleeting look on the girl-woman's face, Arthur quickly agreed, "There must indeed."

Inga's lips twisted. Her eyes darkened and she deliberately changed the subject. "When do we sail?" Eagerness shone in her starlike eyes. "Oh, you can't know what it's been like, all this long time on land."

"Could you ever be happy living on land, Miss Nansen?" Arthur asked. The trivial question took on great importance in his mind.

Inga thoughtfully considered. "I suppose I could, if I were with those I loved." Joyous laughter rang out. "I'd probably be like Ruth in the Bible who followed 'whither.'" Merriment danced in her eyes. "Should Father turn landlubber, so would I, but he'd have to settle me near the water so I could break out now and then." She laughed again and her strong, white teeth flashed. She flung wide her arms in their filmy sleeves. "I want to go everywhere, see everything there is to see. Does that sound strange to you, Dr. Noble?"

"Not at all." He impulsively added, "Have you seen the Alaskan interior?"

Inga's eyes glowed like sapphires. "No, but I hope to one day. Is it as beautiful as they say?" She leaned forward and the gaslight made a halo of her beautiful hair.

"Depending on who 'they' are," he told her. "I'm actually more familiar with Canada than Alaska but I'm planning to head for the Endicott Mountains soon."

Lars broke in. "And I lose the best doctor who ever sailed with me." The corners of his mouth turned down. Before the others could speak, he drew a watch from his pocket. "We'll have time to talk later, Inga. Right now, we need to get you to the Graysons and head back to the ship."

"I'm not going there," she demurely told him. Her mouth twitched. "I've told them and Ruth good-bye and by now my belongings are stowed in my cabin on the *Flower of Alaska*."

Lars threw his hands into the air and hoisted himself from his chair. "I can see the end of peace and quiet on shipboard." He threw down money with a lavish hand, overriding Arthur's protests.

"You old fraud." Drops sparkled in Inga's eyes and she pressed her head against the burly shoulder. "You're just as glad to have me as I am to come."

Lars's sheepishly met Arthur's glance and his grin broadened more than ever.

They reached the docks and Captain Nansen frowned. "Something's strange here." He peered into the gloom. "Where are the watchmen?"

A sense of lurking danger sprang to Arthur's brain but too late. A sudden rush, an outpouring of curses, and heavy bodies flung out of the night onto the men who flanked Inga on either side.

Lars fell beneath the blows from two brawny attackers. "Run!" he yelled in a fear-hoarsened voice.

From his position beneath two others, Arthur thrilled and despaired at Inga's wild, sweet response. "Never!" The voice of her Viking ancestors rang in the darkness. It called forth all the chivalry of the boy who had loved knights battling for their fair ladies. Rage he hadn't realized he possessed lent strength built up by his long years of wandering and the need to survive. Arthur flung a silent prayer for help toward heaven. He twisted his body and with a mighty explosion of muscle and sinew, rolled free. Catlike, he regained his feet and saw Inga valiantly kicking and pounding a fifth man. A split second later his two attackers sprang up and toward him. Arthur threw his arms around one's waist, whirled like a spinning top gone mad, and used the struggling body as a battering ram. It caught the second attacker full force and knocked him off the dock.

Arthur pitched the man he held in a viselike grip after him and turned toward his companions. Inga stood clear. The sound of thudding footsteps showed the cowardly fifth man fleeing after two loud splashes showed his comrades' fate.

Nansen had acquitted himself well. A dark shape lay motionless at his feet and he stood poised to meet his second attacker, who lunged toward him, arm upraised. Dim light gleamed on something in his hand. A boat hook. Lars took a half step backwards, stumbled over the downed thug's body, and fell heavily. With a cry of triumph, the final attacker started forward, murderous weapon ready.

Arthur yelled in pure fury and launched himself in a flying leap that put him between Lars and the hulking brute. He flung up his hands to ward off the blow that would have cracked his skull. He succeeded only in deflecting it, but not enough to save him. The boat hook crashed through the frail protection of upraised hands and tore into Arthur's face.

Agony shot through him. He felt his knees buckle but Inga's screams forced him to remain conscious. He must get up, go to her. His hands felt warm and sticky. He smelled blood.

Another blow fell, followed by the sound of running feet and Lars's cry in the night, "Strongheart!" A plunge into blackness beyond human comprehension. Then—nothing.

❧

Arthur fought his way through an endless black tunnel toward a pinpoint of light so small he wondered if it were real. Was it a ship on the horizon, so faint as to be indiscernible to all but ocean-trained eyes? What made him so tired? His mind churned. He tried to move, but could not. A single twitch of his body sent him back into oblivion. The next time he roused he heard voices.

"Good. He's coming to. Chap's in for a bit of a shock. His face, you know."

Searing memory returned. Darkness. Pain. "Inga?" His shout came out as a slight croak that sounded strange in his ears.

"She is fine. So is Captain Nansen," a calm voice assured. "You got pretty well bunged up but we put you back together again. Did a nice job, too."

Arthur tried to open his eyes. "I can't see!"

"You're bandaged. Cuts on the eyelids but none to the eyes themselves."

New fear spurted. "My hands?"

"No nerves severed, thank God. You'll be operating again in no time."

Relief brought release. Arthur fell back into the pit of silence. He awakened refreshed and struggled to open his eyes. This time he succeeded. His head and hands remained swathed, but not his eyes. A dim light showed the Nansens and a tall, white-clad man with a kindly expression watching him.

"About time you woke up, Dr. Noble. No, don't try to sit

up yet," the stranger warned when Arthur struggled. "You've had a pretty rugged time of it this past week."

"A week? Why, we were supposed to sail."

Lars's face reddened and his eyes shot blue sparks of lightning. "Think we'd sail without you after what you did?" He made a choking sound.

"If you hadn't intervened, the man would have killed Father," Inga said in a low voice. "We can never repay you."

Arthur shook his head. "I don't seem to remember what happened after—"

"Strongheart arrived just in time to save your skin as you saved mine," Lars interjected. "He'd have killed the dirty swine who tried to murder you if the police hadn't come just then." Lars drew in a long sigh. "All five of the men are in jail and likely to be there for a good long time. Seems we aren't the first who've been set on."

The doctor put in, "That's enough. You can come back tomorrow."

He ushered the Nansens out, but not before Arthur whispered, "Tell Strongheart he's repaid me" and caught the pale gleam of Inga's face beneath the braids that had replaced her halo.

"Now. Let's talk turkey." The doctor brought a chair and perched on the edge of it. "Don't be alarmed, but when the bandages come off, you won't look the same."

"You mean—"

"I mean we put your face back together as best we could," the blunt surgeon told him. "But I'm not God and neither are my assistants."

"Then I'll be horribly scarred?" The idea should have terrified him. Instead, Arthur felt glad just to be alive.

"Not at all. I was able to tuck skin flaps with a minimum

of sutures that scarcely show. Your face won't be repulsive, just different. Your voice will remain a tone lower, too. There was just enough damage to alter the sound. All in all, though, you are one lucky man." He rose and stretched.

"How soon can I see myself?"

"Not until I say so," the surgeon barked. "Think I'm going to stand for you to lie there thinking you could have done a better job?" His eyes twinkled. "I'm not saying you couldn't but this is the fanciest piece of suturing I ever did."

Arthur had time to mull over his situation during the time he recuperated. The first thing he decided to do was tell the Nansens the entire story. His lips set in a grim line. Would they cast him off when they learned of the Judas in their midst? He shrugged. So be it. He would sail no more under false colors. Once the bandages came off, he would make full confession to the father and daughter who faithfully refused to sail until he could go with them.

The day Arthur saw himself for the first time since the attack proved climactic. Layer after layer of gauze fell before the snip-snip of the bandage scissors. Arthur had asked that no one but his surgeon be present. When he peered into the mirror offered for his inspection, he gave thanks. A gargoyle stared back, a face to startle any but a trained surgeon. Arthur saw past the swelling and bruises to the end result— and marveled. His face bore little resemblance to the way he once looked but as his doctor predicted, it was not repulsive. As soon as normal healing took place, no one would notice the skillfully hidden repairs.

"One thing," the attending surgeon commented. "With your lower voice and new face, former acquaintances won't know you." He laughed heartily. "You can walk into your best friend's house undetected, if you choose."

A quiver ran through Arthur's veins like a crown fire in August. The hint of an idea came. He rejected it immediately. It returned, again and again. He had a new face. He had a new voice. Why not take advantage of them?

The idea persisted and took hold of him until he began to believe it possible. What if he headed straight for Tarnigan when he healed? Could he pass himself off as someone else just one more time? Hadn't he once dreamed of being able to do just that?

Days later, Arthur came back to the *Flower of Alaska*. The night before she was scheduled to sail, the North Star beckoned in all its glory and a sleepy moon with its eye only half open observed Puget Sound. On the morrow, passengers would crowd the decks and the crew take up their duties. Strongheart, by choice, remained on deck gazing over the water. Only the three companions sat in the tiny sitting room of the captain's quarters. Behind it, three small staterooms housed captain, daughter, and Doctor Noble. Golden lamplight burnished Inga's and Lars's hair and shadowed the girl's flowerlike face.

Arthur took a deep breath. "I have a story to tell you. If after hearing it, you'd rather I not stay aboard, I'll understand." He saw the look of surprise on Lars's face, the convulsive way Inga's fingers tightened on a lace-edged handkerchief.

"My name is not Dr. Noble," he said in his now-husky voice.

"It's Dr. Arthur Baldwin," Lars quietly said.

The doctor straightened. "You know?"

"Yes. You babbled while unconscious." Lars leaned forward, his steady gaze never leaving the younger man's face. "It matters not what you are called. To us, you are Dr. Noble."

"But I'm not!" he cried, oppressed with guilt he believed he'd long since overcome. "I betrayed the best friend I ever had because of jealousy and the mad desire to possess a woman I knew loved no one but herself!" He sprang up and paced the small quarters.

"Once you told me God had forgiven you," Lars reminded. "Have you forgotten that?"

"No." Arthur dropped back to his chair and began to speak. He talked for hours, sparing himself nothing. At times he forgot all but the torment of the past and the remorse that clung to him like a permanent stink. He finished by saying, "I've searched for all these years and grown old in the process." He touched the few streaks of silver at his temples. "I have reason to believe Bern is in a place called Tarnigan."

"Then you must go there." Glorious, free from condemnation, Inga slipped from the chair where she had listened wide-eyed and knelt beside Arthur.

"I shall. The surgeon said even my best friend wouldn't know me. My new voice and face will make it easier."

Inga shrank back in horror, face dead white. "You don't believe God made those monsters assault us, do you?"

Heedless of the watching Lars, Arthur took both of her hands, stood, and raised her to her feet. "Not for a moment! Yet good can come from evil."

She stared at him for a long moment before pulling free. Her color returned. Her eyes sparkled like chips from a glacier. Then a rush of words came that sent both Arthur and the captain into a state of near shock. "Father, will you allow me to go to Tarnigan with Dr. No—Dr. Baldwin?"

eleven

Father, will you allow me go to Tarnigan with Dr. No—Dr. Baldwin?

Had she said those words? Inga gasped at her audacity. How could she have made such an outrageous proposal? Embarrassment waved a color guard in her face. She knew by the sudden heat that swept through her and the incredulous expressions on the men's faces she must be redder than the crimson sky in morning that makes sailors take warning.

Dr. Baldwin recovered his wits first. "Why, I don't see how. It's not that I wouldn't like to have you along, but—" He spread his hands wide, floundering.

"I shouldn't have asked," Inga finally managed in a faint voice. "It's just that I want to go to the interior so badly." Her voice took on unconscious longing. "Forgive me for being ill-mannered, Dr. Baldwin. Of course you can't take me. It's preposterous. My only excuse is a temporary aberration." She turned to Lars and managed a feeble laugh. "Father, this is what comes of clipping my wings and caging me for three long years." She glanced down and miserably traced the grain of the highly polished wooden floor with the toe of her slipper. What must the doctor think of her?

Silence fell like a thunderbolt. When Inga dared look up, the look on her father's face startled her. So did his quiet comment, "It is not preposterous. When folks want to do something badly enough, they usually make a way."

"You mean you'd let me go?" Inga felt torn between

elation and uncertainty. "But how? I mean, I'd need a chaperon and—"

"Perhaps Jean and Fanchon Langlois would be willing to accompany you. Arthur told me they said if the time ever came when they could aid him, all he had to do was ask. Strongheart would go along, of course. Wish I could." Regret showed in his blue eyes. "Tarnigan and its inhabitants sound interesting, whether or not it turns out this Hoots-Noo is Arthur's friend."

Compunction filled her. "Here we've barely had time to get acquainted all over and I'm wanting to leave you." Her voice shook and Inga ran to her father. "I'm sorry."

"I meant what I said, child. If things can be arranged, I see no reason why you should not go." Lars bestowed a look of love on Inga.

Arthur made a muffled sound. His eyes blazed in his pale face. "After what I told you, you'd trust me with your most priceless possession?"

Lars's candid eyes opened wide. "Of course. I can think of no man better equipped to care for my daughter in the same way I would do. Now, do you think you can get Langlois and his wife to agree?"

Arthur nodded. "Yes, unless Fanchon is with child by now. I can send a wire to Fairbanks. A *coureur de bois* will carry the message on fleet feet. It is amazing how rapidly news travels in the wilderness." Excitement etched itself on his features, then a shadow came to darken his eyes.

"There's one hitch. I don't know how long I will have to remain in Tarnigan before making my identity known."

Lars cocked his shaggy head. "If necessary, send Inga back with Jean and Fanchon. Strongheart will want to stay with you, of course." He looked serious. "Perhaps Tarnigan will welcome him and Strongheart will find a home. I have never known a lonelier man." The captain sighed.

"What will you do without me?" Inga demanded. Tears glittered on her long lashes and she almost told him she would stay. A quick glance at Arthur's shining face stilled her protest and drove away the desire to sacrifice the trip.

Lars grimaced. "The same thing I have been doing for three years—only this time it won't be more than three months. Whatever you do, you must not get trapped by snow and ice. I can't spare you for another winter."

"If I did get trapped, I could travel by dogsled," Inga confidently told him. The hair on the nape of her neck raised a bit in anticipation. "I've always wanted to ride one."

"There's nothing more exhilarating," Arthur put in, then stopped short when Lars glared at him. "That is, you don't always ride. Most of the time you run alongside."

"That wouldn't bother her," Lars sourly put in. "She can outrun most men I know. There isn't much she can't do," he grudgingly admitted.

"Including fight." Open admiration showed in Arthur's face and Inga's heart beat so loudly she wondered if the men could hear it.

"What was I supposed to do, stand there and let those men, if you can call them that, pound you to death? I could have fluttered and fainted, I suppose." She raised her voice to a falsetto. "Please, Mr. Bad Men, don't hurt my father and my friend." Her bell-like laugh rang out and she dropped her voice to its normal pitch. "I'm just not a flutterer or a fainter." Did she catch a low "thank God" from Arthur? Inga couldn't be sure and he immediately changed the subject and began to talk about the long trek to Tarnigan.

❧

By the time the *Flower of Alaska* reached Vancouver a terse answer to Arthur's wire awaited them. Jean and Fanchon would meet them at an Indian settlement on the Cook Inlet in southern Alaska, inhabited by Athabaskan, Haida, and Tlingits. "WAIT FOR US," the message concluded.

Inga sometimes felt she would explode with excitement. The beauty of the Inside Passage she had dreamed of since her maiden voyage three years before thrilled her more than ever. Fair hair swept back in thick braids, the wind in her face, the last of the hurt instilled by Byron Irving fled. She caught herself watching Arthur Baldwin while he busied himself with a hundred tasks about ship. Her capable hands provided valuable assistance. So did all she had learned at the university. Arthur often said she and Strongheart made the best team of helpers any surgeon could desire. How could she have thought herself even mildly in love with the bogus professor when such a man as this ship's doctor walked the earth? She cringed and thanked God Ruth Perkins had been right. Wounded pride healed far sooner than a wounded heart.

Long before they reached the meeting place, Inga realized her heart had winged its way to "Dr. Noble," as Lars sometimes still called him. She hid the knowledge as best she could but one quiet evening when dusk painted the horizon with fog-gray, her father gently laid a hand on her shoulder.

"It's all right, Inga. He is a good man."

She started and felt color flood to her face. "I—I don't know if he cares." The fear she carried came out in the frankness she and her father always shared. He often likened her to Nathanael of old, whom Jesus said was without guile.

"He cares, daughter. You are more precious to him than life itself." A sweet smile curved Lars's lips. Inga knew he saw far beyond the horizon, to a place where his beloved

Astrid awaited his coming. Lars continued in a husky, emotion-charged tone, "I have prayed for God to spare me until I see you safely in harbor with one who loves Him. Inga my own, should you and Arthur join your lives, I will embark on my last journey content."

Inga slipped a hand through Lars's stalwart arm and leaned against him, too deeply moved for words. At last she spoke into the encroaching darkness. "Father, are you not well?"

His great laugh boomed out. "I am hale and hearty and expect to live long enough to see children and grandchildren playing on the deck."

The fragile moment closed but Inga knew the blessed memory would remain with her forever. Why, then, did an odious little worry prompt her to whisper, "He has said nothing."

"Nor should he," Lars promptly told her. "Our good doctor must complete his quest before seeking the fair lady's favor." His light tone didn't mask the seriousness of his evaluation or the subtle warning in what he said.

"Then I will wait." Inga smiled.

"It is good. Always men must conquer while women wait," Lars gruffly told her and shook his brawny shoulders in a gesture that spoke louder than words.

Each day brought them closer to the meeting place with the Langloises. A growing impatience to be there in no way hindered Inga from fully enjoying the scenery along the way. She thrilled to Sitka, founded by the Russian trader Alexander Baranof in 1799 and originally named New Archangel, and now, since 1884, the capital of Alaska. "Although Juneau has recently been designated as the new capital," Lars explained. "It will take time to relocate."

At last the meeting place hove into view before Inga's

wondering eyes. It lay in the shadow of the Chugach Mountains. Inga had never seen such flowers and fruit as those that grew in this protean land with its snowcapped peaks and fertile valleys. She gazed shoreward, eager to catch a glimpse of Jean and Fanchon Langlois, with whom she would be associating for many weeks.

"They probably won't be here yet," Arthur warned. "They had a long way to travel." He smiled and his eyes glistened. "You will love them, Inga." The more formal *Miss Nansen* had disappeared more completely than the occasional whales the party saw as they steamed north.

"Will they like me?" She hadn't even considered it before. How terrible if they proved uncongenial.

"What's not to like?" Lars ruffled up like a turkey whose feathers had been disturbed.

Arthur's high spirits bubbled over. "Well, right now she has a patch of flour on her forehead the exact shape of Whidbey Island," he teased. "Otherwise, she's nearly perfect." The warmth in his face outdid even that in his voice.

Inga blushed and pretended indignation. "What an ungrateful wretch! And after I spent all morning baking pies," she exclaimed, but couldn't help laughing. A lightning swipe removed the smudge even though Arthur quickly said he found it mighty becoming.

≈

Contrary to his predictions, the Langloises had arrived the afternoon before the *Flower of Alaska* anchored in deep water. Lars, Arthur, and Inga rowed ashore. For some strange reason Strongheart chose to remain on the ship. He had grown quieter than ever as the boat steamed north. Now he merely said, "I will meet them when they board the ship." Inga exchanged puzzled glances with Arthur but neither protested.

Respect for the Indian precluded their attempting to change his mind once he had made it up.

Surrounded by trees and lush grass, the two sets of travelers met against a backdrop worthy of the finest stage play. The slim French Canadian couple looked no more fatigued than if they had left their home hundreds of miles north only that morning. "Ah, *M'sieu*," Jean exclaimed, fingers gripping the doctor's in a steely hold. "You are well and that is good."

Inga didn't miss the keen glance he sent from Arthur's face to her own, nor the shier but equally welcoming look that flashed from pretty Fanchon's eyes.

"Oh, but it is good to meet you," Inga cried. "Dr. Baldwin has told me so much, I feel as if I already know you."

"Dr. Baldwin?" Jean looked mystified.

"My real name," Arthur explained. "I picked up the Dr. Noble moniker in my travels."

"*Oui*." Jean nodded. "Dr. Noble Baldwin has told us nothing about you," he pointedly added. His white teeth flashed into a mischievous smile. "I wonder why that is."

Inga delightedly watched a red tide flow into Arthur's face but Fanchon tranquilly said, "My Jean, always a joke he makes. Miss Nansen, I am glad we meet."

"Call me Inga, please." She felt herself throwing off shackles of Seattle propriety. What mattered it they'd met only moments before? She had a feeling of sisterhood with the lovely girl who stood before her.

Lars's mighty paw engulfed Jean's, then Fanchon's. "We must talk. I have an idea." He shook his head mysteriously when Inga raised her eyebrows. "Not yet, daughter. First we go to the *Flower of Alaska*." He turned back to the Langloises. "She has been baking pies and our cook is preparing a salmon Dr. Baldwin took from the sea this very morning."

Jean's eyes glistened. "Ah, she cooks and is beautiful, as well. Just like my Fanchon." His hand rested on his wife's heavy black braid that hung in front of one buckskin-clad shoulder. His open, loving look sent a pang into Inga's heart. If only Arthur would one day look so at her, proudly announcing to all the world he cared not a whit what it thought so long as his wife stood by his side.

They boarded the ship, Lars first, then Inga, Fanchon, Arthur and Jean last. Strongheart stood to one side, making no effort to join the group until summoned in Lars's usual hearty manner. "Langlois, Fanchon, meet our friend Strongheart."

"*Strongheart!*" Jean Langlois whipped around, eyes glittering. His voice fell to a strangled whisper. "It can't be possible."

The first real smile the Nansens or Arthur had ever seen on the Indian's impassive face spread across chiseled features, softening them into beauty.

"But you are dead!" Jean staggered back. "I myself saw you die more than twenty years ago." He passed a shaking hand over his eyes.

"No. You saw me go over the falls," Strongheart corrected. "The rapids and rocks chewed at me until they tired of their sport. Then they spit me out on the bank of the river miles below." He shrugged. "A squaw found and cared for me."

Great drops stood on Jean's face. He wordlessly gripped Strongheart's hand. Face working, he explained brokenly, "Forgive me. All these years I thought the man who saved a small boy from drowning lost his life in the greedy river. Strongheart, where have you been?"

Life went from the Indian's face and he dropped Jean's hand. "Many places." The next moment he turned on his heel and strode away on silent, moccasined feet. He paused beside the rail a short distance away.

"That's all you'll ever get out of him," Fanchon observed. Her dark eyes looked enormous in the pale tan oval of her face. "*M'essieurs, mademoiselle,* how is it Strongheart is with you?"

Arthur explained briefly and lowered his voice. "Who is he, anyway?"

"He is Strongheart." Jean shook his head sadly. "No one knows from where he came. I never heard more of him after he rescued me from my foolishness before I was ten. Maman warned me about the river, but I thought I could wade across as I had seen my older brothers and sisters do. I chose a time when my family were all busy elsewhere. I didn't want to be seen and stopped." He mopped sweat from his forehead. "The current knocked me down. No one was there to hear my cries." He shuddered and Inga knew his memories remained clear after all the long years.

Jean hastily crossed himself but his skin remained blanched. "I knew it would be an awful thing to face the great God and have to say, 'Jean Langlois is here because he did not obey his maman.' Yet I cried out to Him for help. Strong arms grabbed me and I asked, 'Are you, God?'" A mystic look stole into Jean's eyes. "My rescuer said no, he was only Strongheart. Somehow he fought his way to the edge of the river." Anguish made Jean look old.

"Coughing and sputtering, I felt his hold on me loosen. He flung me to the shore, then disappeared into the churning water, spent from the terrible effort of saving me. I screamed for him to come back. He did not." Horror returned to the storyteller's features. "I saw him go over the falls. All these years, I knew he died because I disobeyed. It has been a heavy burden, one even my Fanchon did not know I carried."

His shaken wife stared at him, then rose and ran to Strongheart, grace in every movement of her fluid body. She threw her arms around the Indian, leaned against his chest and sobbed. "Thank you."

Inga felt her throat tighten, her eyes sting at the unreadable expression on the Indian's face. He awkwardly patted the shining braid. Fanchon's sobs finally ceased. She raised her head, stood on tiptoe, and touched Strongheart's cheek with tear-wet lips.

He stepped back with an incoherent cry. One hand touched his face, then he turned and ran from Fanchon as if she were a wild beast bent on destroying him.

Inga felt her heart full to bursting. With a hasty apology she slipped away to her tiny cabin space, fell to her knees, and thanked God for the mysterious Indian who had affected each of their lives. Then, like a true Scandinavian hostess, she dried her tears and went to see to the comfort of her guests.

❧

"Strongheart," Lars called to the Indian standing by the rail after dinner ended and the Nansens, Langloises, and Arthur gathered on deck. "How well do you know Alaska?"

"Well." The Indian had regained his usual composure. He stood with arms crossed over his chest.

"I've been thinking. Wouldn't it be shorter for our expedition to go inland to Tarnigan from the coast north of Nome than back the way the Langloises came?"

"Much, but the land is rugged." Strongheart raised one eyebrow.

"More rugged than crossing the Alaska Range between here and Fairbanks?"

Strongheart shook his head. "There are fewer trails."

Lars's eyes gleamed. "What if we sail from here south past Kodiak Island—"

"The Russians formed the first white settlement there in 1784," Jean put in.

"From there we'd go southeast to Unalaska and the Fox Islands, steam into the Bering Sea, and head north. Are there Indian coastal villages where a man can barter for furs?" Lars wanted to know. "Now that Nome's overrun with gold seekers, the fur trade may have dwindled."

Interest stirred in Strongheart's face. "Perhaps. How much past Nome do you wish to go? Through the Bering Strait? You'll face treacherous waters but just across the Arctic Circle, a sound lies due west of the Endicott Mountains."

"I don't know that country," Jean frankly admitted. "Strongheart, you'll have to guide us if we go that way." Respect and anticipation brightened his face.

The Indian looked from person to person. Last of all, his gaze rested on Inga. She felt herself measured, weighed. The dead blackness of his eyes softened. "The trail is long and hard, but I will take you to Tarnigan." He turned, faced north, and fell silent as the clusters of stars in the inverted bowl of heaven above.

twelve

Flickering flames lighted and shadowed five faces in turn. Somewhere in the distance a wolf called for his mate. Stars the size of a man's fist hung low over the diverse group of travelers welded together by hardship and dependence on one another. Weary horses freed from saddles and gear snorted and rolled in the grass beneath their feet, then quietly grazed in their hastily constructed rope corral. Thanks to Captain Nansen, Strongheart's party enjoyed as much comfort as a well-equipped outfit could provide.

Arthur Baldwin leaned back on one elbow and surveyed his companions. As usual, Strongheart stood tall and impassive a little to one side. He had changed in the days since they bade Captain Nansen farewell and watched the *Flower of Alaska* sail without them. His command of the group necessitated giving directions and the others' eager questions lessened his reticence. On occasion, the rare smile that so changed his appearance crept over his bronzed face. A wave of kinship for the outcast filled Arthur. He, too, knew what it meant to walk alone. God grant that both he and Strongheart might find peace in Tarnigan.

Arthur's gaze rested on Jean Langlois and his Fanchon, seated next to one another on a blanket while Jean whistled a lively chanson of the north. Sometimes he sang in French, slightly off key. Although the doctor didn't understand a word, he knew it for a love song by the expression in Fanchon's lovely eyes.

136

Last of all, Arthur looked at Inga. She had adopted Fanchon's hairstyle, and her thick blonde braid hung in front of one shoulder. It became her well. Little golden tendrils escaped from their confinement and curled around her face.

A great surge of joy brought Arthur to his feet and he paced in front of the fire. If he were not mistaken, the first shy signs of love showed now and then in Inga's fjord-blue eyes when she thought he wasn't looking. His blood raced. God willing, one day she would walk with him as Fanchon did with Jean, two against the world, loving one another and serving their Master.

"*M'sieu* did not get enough exercise today?" Jean innocently inquired. He cocked his dark head to one side and gleams of mischief danced in his eyes. "He prowls like the wolf searching for his mate."

Fanchon giggled. Strongheart said nothing, but his lips twitched. Inga continued to stare into the fire. Arthur couldn't tell if her face reddened at the sally. He knew his own did. Confound Langlois and his keen perception!

"Is that what I look like?" he forced himself to say. "I shaved this morning so I shouldn't be shaggy like your friend the wolf." He dropped back to the ground.

Jean started to speak, but Fanchon shot a quick glance at Inga and softly asked, "Strongheart, we have come through low, rolling hills and broad swampy river valleys. What must we conquer next?"

"Tomorrow we turn north toward the Endicotts," their guide said in his resonant voice.

"They're part of the Brooks Range, are they not?"

Strongheart nodded. "Yes. The Brooks Range extends to the Arctic Ocean."

"I thought we'd be on tundra," Arthur said.

Strongheart's face broke into a small smile. "The tundra is north of the Continental Divide. The Endicotts and Tarnigan are south."

"What is tundra like? Have you been there?"

The Indian's eyes halfclosed. "It is a land beautiful as a false-hearted woman." A ripple of surprise ran around the circle but Strongheart continued. "The ground deep beneath the plain remains frozen, year after year, century after century. Trees cannot grow." A dreaming look filled his dark face. His voice softened. "Many men who were foolish enough to go there in winter have died from lack of food and shelter. Summer changes everything. The surface of the ground thaws. Sleeping grass awakens and forms a thick carpet. Wild flowers spring up. For a short season, the land lives in beauty. Then it dies."

A shadow fell over Strongheart's face and chilled the night air. Arthur couldn't bear the desolation he sensed rather than saw in the other. "Yet it lives again," Arthur said.

"Yes."

Challenged, Arthur added, "Just like man."

Strongheart turned questioning eyes toward the doctor. "Does man live again? I do not know. Perhaps he becomes as the wind, forever crying in the night. Those who taught me did not know, either. Some said man went back to dust." He raised his head and looked to the North Star. "Others said this life was not the end."

He fixed his gaze on Arthur. "I would like to believe we are as important as the flower that blooms, dies, and lives again. So far I cannot. If it is true, if there is a better world to come, why do men toil and sweat for gold in this one? Why do they steal and kill and destroy? And why do fathers desert their wives and children?"

The impassioned words cut Arthur to the heart. He prayed for the right words. None came.

Inga rose and stood before Strongheart. Firelight glowed in her hair and turned it to a halo. Her eyes became deep, mysterious wells of midnight blue. "We are more important than grass and flowers and trees, Strongheart. Did your teachers not tell you God created us in His own image? Or that He loved us so much He sent the only Son He would ever have to die so we might live with Him forever?"

"This I have heard."

"It is true." Inga's gaze never wavered. Arthur's heart thumped. He longed to cry out affirmation but something prevented his doing so, perhaps unwillingness to break the fragile thread spinning itself between Inga and Strongheart.

"How do you know?" the tall man demanded. "Have you seen this God?"

"Have you seen the wind?" she countered.

He silently shook his head.

"Yet you know it exists. You have stood on high mountains and exulted at its force. You have ridden the *Flower of Alaska* in angry seas and marveled it did not break in two. You know there is a wind because you have felt it and witnessed what it can do." Inga clasped both hands to her breast. "Strongheart, I know God for the same reasons."

After a long moment Strongheart said, "You speak well."

"They are not my words, good friend, but His." Inga laid a hand on his sleeve and tipped her head back to look into his face. "Don't let those who follow the evil one keep you from the One who sacrificed so much that we might live."

Arthur trembled. *God,* he pleaded in his soul, *help this troubled man come to You. And please, give me the opportunity to tell Bern about Your love.*

Strongheart gently removed Inga's hand. He bowed, backed away, and disappeared into the night without a single footfall to show the way he went. A gossamer sigh circled the campfire and at last Jean said, *"Oui, mademoiselle*, you speak well." He gracefully rose, took Fanchon by the hand, and raised her to her feet. "Tomorrow is a long day. We must rest."

Long after Inga and Fanchon had retired to the silken tent they shared and Jean slept rolled in a blanket by the fire, Arthur sat staring into the dying embers. The memory of Strongheart's outburst haunted him. Never before had the Indian opened his heart in such a way. Perhaps he never would again. Yet tonight four people had seen into the depths of a man who struggled with an unknown past.

Hours passed. The guide did not return. The northern moon shone pitilessly down on the little camp and still Arthur did not sleep. At last he slipped from his blankets and stole away into the night, asking God to guide him. A half hour later his heart leaped with joy. Strongheart stood a hundred or so yards away, leaning against a lightning-scarred tree trunk. The symbolism touched Arthur. Both had known terrible jolts. Could either survive? Yes. New growth had already formed at the base of the tree trunk.

He paused, wondering if Strongheart would resent his coming. The magnificent head turned slightly. "Come."

He slowly went forward and took his position next to his friend. What could he say or do to bring Christ into this hurting man's world? A voice rang in his soul, clearer than the bugle of an elk: *Confess your past and tell him you are forgiven.*

God, how can I? Arthur silently argued. Lars said Strongheart may very well be part white. If I confess what I did, he will despise me. I will lose all chance of bringing him to You.

Tell him.

In fear and obedience Arthur said, "Strongheart, I have a story you must hear." He felt the other man stiffen and his heart quailed until a voice from long ago came to give him strength. Lars Nansen, saying, "A man must follow his proddings." Certainty overwhelmed him. If this prodding were of God, remaining silent meant turning his back on the promptings of the Holy Spirit.

Arthur began his story in halting, broken tones. He sketched in his brotherhood with Bern Clifton, the cheerful rivalry that spurred each to do his best until Julia dawned on the horizon. He dared not look at the rigid man beside him, frozen as a glacier in winter. When Arthur confessed his betrayal and its tragic results, a single sound came from Strongheart's lips: the low cry of one in mortal pain, followed by a convulsive start Arthur realized meant the prelude to flight.

"You must hear me out," he cried. His hand closed on the Indian's muscle-hard arm. "I have endured agony. There is no place on earth for a Judas." Memory of all the months and years he suffered rang in the moonlit night.

Strongheart uttered no further sound. Neither did he leave.

Arthur's hand fell to his side and he continued. He told of Benjamin Clifton and his great heart that held no malice. Of Donal' MacDonal', who loved God's children and gave his life to them. He briefly touched on his efforts to reestablish contact with his parents and how he failed. In sparse words, Arthur painted a portrait of the past years and how the encounter with Jean Langlois had restored hope that had almost died.

"Perhaps Hoots-Noo is not Bern Clifton," he finished. "I will know soon."

Strongheart spoke for the first time. "And if he is?"

Arthur heard a note of suspended judgment. "He will not recognize me. I will have opportunity to know him. One day, when the time is right, I will tell him of the long journey I have traveled to find him."

"Why do you do this thing? He may not forgive you." Strongheart peered at Arthur in the predawn gloom that came when the moon slid behind a tall mountain in the distance. "You say your God has forgiven you. Why does it matter if your enemy continues to hold hatred in his heart?"

An unexplainable sense of something beyond his ken caused Arthur to say, "My only enemy was pride. I cannot be responsible for Bern shutting God out of his life because of my sins. If I do, I am no better than those who have robbed you of something more precious than gold."

Had he gone too far? he wondered. Surely not. The words had not been of himself.

An eternity later the other said, "It was not easy for you to tell me these things. Why did you confess?"

"I could do nothing else."

Strongheart's hand gripped his. "You are a good man."

Arthur returned the clasp with all his might. "I am a weak man who deserved no mercy, loved by God, who never gave up on me. Everything Inga told you is true. Will you think about it?"

Strongheart freed his hand and stepped away. Dawn's stretching white fingers found his face and rested there. His chiseled features resumed their usual reserve and Arthur's spirits dragged to the ground until his companion muttered, "Perhaps," and strode toward the direction of camp.

Feeling he had won at least a skirmish in what surely would be a long, hard war, Arthur followed.

A few days later they reached the Endicotts. Arthur longed to speed up. Strongheart refused. "We must travel into the mountains," he said. "I have not been to Tarnigan but I know what to expect on the way there. It will take all your stamina." A fleeting smile twitched at his lips. "One does not become a good rider in a day."

Arthur laughed ruefully and so did Inga. The Langloises had no problem with horseback travel but the two Americans found themselves stiff in spite of frequent stops for rest. "You win," he told their guide and sighed. The closer he got to his destination, the more he wondered. Would his altered appearance deceive the coal-black eyes of the man he had once called brother?

The terrain changed. Fragrant, cool, green forest closed around them. Its magic gripped the riders. When Inga turned her attention from the damp trail that wound between silver-trunked birch trees and looked to the side, Arthur saw in her face the same wonder he felt. The horses' hooves made no sound in the wet mold of the trail. Neither was there sound or echo of sound between earth and sky. Arthur had a feeling the silence was ancient as the hills themselves, haunted by a spirit of holiness.

He winced when his knee hit adjacent tree trunks with a resounding thwack and concentrated more on riding, less on his surroundings. Once or twice a young sapling bent forward by Inga's horse snapped back, but he managed to avoid it. The trail narrowed. Moss-grown logs impeded their progress.

"Kick your horses in the ribs when you come to a high log," Strongheart advised. "They must clear the logs in a single jump or they will lose their footing and fall."

The trail steepened. A river lay far below like a silver thread in a tapestry of green. Natural meadows, ever-changing clouds, long slopes, and lone aspens left the travelers speechless. How grand it would be in autumn, with the coming winter painting gold leaves that quivered as they passed! Arthur took in a hurting breath. By autumn, Inga would be gone. And he? Only God knew the answer to that question.

Now the path demanded his full attention, so steep Strongheart ordered them to walk. Ridges and passes, shadowy vales and grassy slopes. All called to Arthur's sense of beauty in a way foreign to his early years in the city. Again the look in Inga's eyes when she smiled back at him over her shoulder showed she shared his sense of aliveness.

"This is one of the grandest parts of Alaska," Jean called from his position behind Fanchon and in front of Inga. "And one of the few I hadn't seen." A rakish leaf clung to his mussed hair but didn't detract from his white smile. "I think maybe my Fanchon and I will return, once we see *Mademoiselle* Inga safely back to her father."

Dismay spoiled some of Arthur's pleasure. He remembered Inga's comment about needing the sea to be happy, even though she also said joy came from being with those one loved. When the time came to tell her he cherished her above all else on earth, would she find enough love in her heart to go "whither" with him, as she laughingly called it?

"Tarnigan is below."

Strongheart's calm voice broke into Arthur's troubled soliloquy. He reined in his mount on the top of the rise. Before him lay a long green valley, guarded by jutting white peaks and mountain ranges' sheer sides. Spruce clumps, silver streams, lakes as sapphire as Inga's eyes, cottonwood thickets, churning white waterfalls spit from cracked hills, and parklike openings spread their panorama. Arthur heard Inga gasp. He urged his horse forward to a wide spot in the trail and looked into her face, then wrenched his gaze away, feeling he had seen into the holy of holies.

In silence they descended, a blazing sunset to their left and the chill of night blowing down on them from snowy peaks. Even the loquacious Jean appeared subdued by the wild land into which they had come. Fanchon's eyes looked bigger than ever and she urged her horse forward until its nose nearly touched the tail of Strongheart's mount, who led the way.

"Is it any wonder *M'sieu* Nicolai Anton named his home *Nika Illahee?*" Jean finally breathed.

"What does it mean?" Inga's voice sounded hushed as befitted the fading day.

" 'My dear homeland.' "

Arthur pondered it as they reached the valley floor; even more so when he caught sight of dusky forms he knew must be the Indians Anton loved and tried so hard to protect from the evils of whisky given by degenerate whites. No wonder the people of the north called Nicolai and his daughter Sasha angels! His heart pounded. Had Bern stayed, perhaps married "Little Flower" as her father called her? Or had the unworthy Ivan Romanov won her? Months had gone by since Jean had heard from the brother whom the Antons had taken in and cared for.

A well-lighted building ahead brought a grunt from Strongheart and quickened the pace of the horses. Not far away, a log home Arthur realized must be *Nika Illahee* sparkled with lamp and firelight, visible through a

wide-swung door and shining windows. The sound of a
woman's laugh floated out, then a hearty chuckle. For one
terrifying moment Arthur turned craven and he longed to
flee.

A man stepped to the porch. "Hello, there."

The long-remembered voice sent sweat to Arthur's forehead. His hands trembled. The one factor he hadn't counted
on, the single element he never dreamed would appear, stood
waiting on the porch. Not Bern, who hadn't seen him in
years, but—

"Anton?" Strongheart called.

"He is away." The familiar voice beat into Arthur's brain.
"Welcome."

Somehow he got off his horse and into a brilliantly lighted
room. Worst fears confirmed, Arthur looked straight into
Benjamin Clifton's face.

thirteen

Your best friend won't know you, the Seattle surgeon had said. Now Arthur faced his first test. Pale but determined, he faced Benjamin Clifton, noting with a professional eye how much better the older man looked than on their last meeting. The peace in his face showed his coming to Tarnigan must have brought reconciliation with his son. Hope sprang into Arthur's heart and a fervent prayer that he, too, might be forgiven.

Benjamin greeted the other travelers and turned to Arthur, hand outstretched, a puzzled expression in his eyes. "You are?"

"They call me Noble." Identity on trial, the doctor held his breath.

Clifton started, peered at him, then shook his head. "For a moment I thought I recognized you, but—"

"This is my first trip to Tarnigan," Arthur said in his altered voice. He deliberately made his handshake brief.

Jean Langlois broke in. "*M'sieu,* my brother was here some time ago. Did he remain? I have not heard for a long time." He repeated his brother's name.

Clifton shook his head. "I believe he's gone trapping. Anton mentioned him. If you stay here long, you should see him when he brings his furs in. Anton is a fur trader, you know, as well as owner of the trading post."

Jean's eyes gleamed in the lamplight of the pleasant room. "*Oui.* There is much trapping here?" The conversation drifted into a discussion of the many fur-bearing animals in the area. Several times Arthur caught Benjamin's furtive gaze and decided to tell him the truth the first moment they had alone.

His time did not come that night. Nicolai Anton and two dark-haired girls who looked enough alike to be sisters burst in, followed by a perfectly marked Malamute. "Down, Kobuk," Anton shouted when the dog growled low in his throat. "You must forgive him," the big man apologized. "He's been trained to guard Little Flower and Naleenah and guard he does." His shout of laughter reminded Arthur of Lars Nansen. "I am Nicolai Anton. This is my daughter Sasha—now Mrs. Bern Clifton. And my adopted daughter Naleenah."

Arthur stared at the smiling young woman with sparkling dark hair and slightly slanted brown eyes. Bern's wife? How Julia Langley's pallid prettiness faded by comparison with this flower of the north! "Your husband is to be congratulated," Arthur told her from the bottom of his heart.

Sasha's face flamed a clear red. "Thank you, *M'sieu*." She bobbed a quaint curtsey, then slipped her arm through Naleenah's. "Come. We must prepare food for these travelers. They look as starved as I am." A little frown marred her forehead. "Father Benjamin, where is that husband of mine?"

"Kayak Jim spirited him away to patch up a broken head. Someone smuggled whisky into the Indian village again and a fight broke out."

Anton bellowed like a gunshot grizzly. "Has that skunk Ivan come back?"

Arthur saw Naleenah's face pale, the quick way she tensed. He had no time to ponder it. A hiss so low only he could hear it turned his attention to Strongheart. The guide's pupils had dwindled to tiny dots and he stared at Naleenah.

Suspicion attacked. Arthur immediately rejected it as impossible. The long arm of coincidence couldn't stretch from Ketchikan to Tarnigan, could it? Yet he'd never seen such hatred in Strongheart's face.

"Who is Ivan? Where has he been?" Arthur asked.

"Ivan Romanov, my former trusted associate," Anton heavily said. Great furrows lined his formerly laughing face. "All the time he ran the trading post for me he smuggled whisky to the Indian village. He also robbed my fur cache and attempted to steal Sasha, then Naleenah. We drove him away months ago. Rumor said Ivan had been seen in Juneau and Prince Rupert, then we heard no more." A bitter laugh hung in the smoke-fragrant air. "I didn't believe he'd dare return. It can only mean he seeks revenge."

Arthur's thoughts whirled. Ketchikan lay between Juneau and Prince Rupert. A lightning glance at Strongheart confirmed suspicion. Inconceivable as it might be, Ivan Romanov was the man who beat and left him for dead. It blazed in Strongheart's smoldering stare, still fixed on the distraught Naleenah. She looked up, as though compelled by the intent gaze. Something flickered behind the fear in her eyes. The next moment Sasha gently tugged her arm and they disappeared through a door at the side of the room.

Arthur turned back to Strongheart. A poignant light slowly replaced ugliness born of hate, then he assumed his usual emotionless expression. The doctor felt shaken. What complications had he created by bringing Strongheart to Tarnigan? Lars had hoped the Indian would find peace there. Now it appeared each person present would be embroiled in a fight of good versus evil, in the person of Ivan Romanov. Not Inga, Arthur decided. Jean and Fanchon must take her back. His heart protested with every beat. He could not let her go. Neither could he have her stay and be exposed to the undercurrents that swirled in Tarnigan.

Shaken by the revelation, the entrance of two men caught Arthur unprepared for the moment he had anticipated, feared, and dreaded for years. A leathery man, prototype of all the prospectors Arthur had stumbled across in his travels, stepped into the room. A tall, proud man followed.

"Where's Sasha?" he demanded in the rich, laughing tone Arthur had never forgotten. He threw down his medical bag. "Fine thing. A man slaves away to earn money for his wife and she hides when the master of the house comes home. What kind of wife is she?" he asked the assembled group. Love shone in his soot-black eyes. Silver wings more pronounced than those at Arthur's temples brightly streaked his black hair.

A rush of flying feet brought Sasha to her husband's side. From the circle of his arms she introduced their guests. Dr. Clifton responded with a bow to Fanchon, a hearty handshake for each of the men.

Arthur hung back, calling on all his medical training to compose himself in the short time remaining. He hadn't known it would be like this. A great tearing inside threatened to rend his heart in two.

Sasha's soft voice cut into his Gethsemane. "This is *M'sieu* Noble."

"Noble? You remind me of someone." Bern shook hands and looked puzzled, as his father had done earlier. His brows met and formed a straight, black line above his craggy face. "Where are you from?"

Arthur slowly replied, "I've been sailing with Captain Lars Nansen on the *Flower of Alaska*." Thank God his comrades had agreed to call him Noble.

His changed voice passed muster. Bern dropped his hand, an unreadable look in his keen eyes. Regret? Disappointment? "I must be mistaken. The man I knew wouldn't be caught dead west of Philadelphia."

That man is gone forever, Arthur wanted to shout. The one who stands before you is as far removed from the arrogant doctor you knew as is Boston from Tarnigan. He held his tongue, trying to decipher what he had seen in Bern's face when he said he must be mistaken.

"There are empty houses in the village or we have room for you to stay here," Anton hospitably invited after they ate. Naleenah and Sasha, aided by an insistent Inga, served a caribou roast that had been slowly browning all afternoon, a surprising array of fresh, home-grown vegetables, and apple pies dusted with sugar.

"Miss Nansen—Inga—will stay with us," Sasha announced. "So will the Langloises."

"I'd be proud to have Noble and Strongheart at my shack," Kayak Jim drawled. His eyes twinkled. "If'n they c'n put up with an old prospector."

"Shack!" Sasha exploded. "He has one of the prettiest places in Tarnigan. We finally convinced him he needed somewhere to call home when he got tired of looking for gold." Her laugh sang like a trickling stream. "Besides, he found enough a long time ago to keep him the rest of his life."

Strongheart acted startled at the invitation. Arthur knew few whites had treated him as an equal. When they reached Kayak's so-called shack, the Indian looked ready to bolt. Built on the same general plan as *Nika Illahee*, the log home commanded a fine view of mountains and valley.

"The gals fixed it up," the old prospector muttered,

waving at turkey-red calico curtains and pillows heaped high on a hand-hewn couch. He led his guests to adjoining rooms, whitewashed and simple but made attractive with more curtains plus bright patchwork quilts on narrow beds. "Make y'rselves t'home."

Bathed and eager, the guests gathered in front of a blazing open fireplace despite the lateness of the hour. Arthur encouraged their host to tell all he knew of Ivan Romanov, the Indian village, and the Antons's work. He thrilled when he learned how Bern once saved Kayak's life, to be rewarded with riches by the grateful prospector. The next morning he sought out Benjamin Clifton and confessed who he really was.

"I wanted to get to know Bern as he is now," Arthur said with bowed head. "Am I wrong?"

Benjamin laid a fatherly hand on his head. "You will know in your heart when the time is right to speak. I believe my son has forgiven you long ago, before he became a follower of Christ. Sometimes he mentions you. I find no bitterness in him."

Arthur had to turn away to hide the freshet that sprang forth. He also had a private and fateful talk with Inga and the Langloises. Strongheart stood in the background, as usual. "I will stay," Arthur told them simply. "You must go. According to Kayak, there is great danger."

A scornful flash of blue eyes greeted his pronouncement. Inga's lips curled. "No Nansen ever ran away from trouble. Neither shall I."

"Your father entrusted you to my care," Arthur protested, although his heart thrilled with admiration for her courage, fear for her safety.

"I am Inga, hero's daughter," she retorted. "My father would despise me if I turned my back on those who need help so badly. Sasha told me this Ivan Romanov hounded her and Naleenah like the worst kind of cur. He vowed to get even with Nicolai and Dr. Clifton. You ask me to think of myself? Never!"

Arthur looked to the Langloises for support. He received none.

"Do not look at me, *M'sieu* Noble," Jean told him. "Has not Jean Langlois fought the bear, the wolf, the mountain lion? Pah!" He snapped his fingers. "Who is this Russian to put fear into our hearts?"

"Fanchon?"

"My Jean and I are strong," she quietly said. "We can fight, if necessary."

Arthur turned to Strongheart, his last hope. "Tell them how evil this man is."

A dozen emotions played over the still face before he spoke. "Why do you fear evil? Is your God so weak he will allow wicked men to destroy the great good these people do here in Tarnigan?" His voice rolled out like a prophet of old. "Miss Nansen has spoken. Captain Nansen would expect us to stay."

Arthur raised his hands in a gesture of defeat. "So be it," he grimly told them. Thirty minutes later he announced their decision to the brave little band attempting to stop the tide of wickedness from again wreaking havoc on their village and saw the relief in five pairs of watching eyes.

The decision came none too soon. Three days later, rifle shots spanged from a thicket near *Nika Illahee* and buried themselves in the log walls.

"Thank God no one was hurt," Arthur exclaimed.

"The marksman wasn't shooting to kill," Bern Clifton

hoarsely said. "If he had been. . ." He shrugged, his meaning clear. "Romanov isn't desperate enough to risk such a move, although it may come to that." His burning gaze circled the group. "Anyone want to reconsider staying?" He looked at Inga and Fanchon.

"Not I." Inga tossed her blonde braid back and the light of battle came to her eyes. Fanchon murmured assent.

Arthur saw the same deep admiration he held for Inga spring to Bern's eyes. "We stay," he vowed and felt kinship renew when Bern again clasped his hand.

Several quiet days passed. Arthur had time to walk with Inga, Jean with his Fanchon, although Bern warned them not to get out of sight of Tarnigan. "Romanov's susceptible to pretty women," he warned. "Once he gets sight of Inga and Fanchon, who knows what mischief he may do? He's still holding a grudge about Sasha and Naleenah. God help any woman he gets in his power."

His somber cautions and the threat of what surely lay ahead could not withstand summer in Tarnigan. Love abounded in field and forest. Bucks and does proudly displayed spotted fawns. Birds hatched in the spring learned to fly. The northern sun kissed the land and promised constancy, although in a few months fall and winter would ruthlessly dim its warmth. Wild flowers nodded. Aspens bent to one another and whispered secrets.

On the loveliest day of all, Arthur declared his love. "I planned to wait," he huskily said. "Now we don't know what is ahead. Inga, one day when all this is over and I have completed my atonement, will you be my wife?"

Color stained her fair face, as fresh as the Indian paintbrush blossoming at the foot of the great rock where they sat. She stared at him, then opened her lips to reply.

Arthur forestalled her. "Before you answer, consider well." He turned from her clear, blue eyes to the smiling land around them. "I don't know where God may call me to serve. It may not always be on the *Flower of Alaska*, or even near the sea you love, that is so much a part of you. I want you to be happy, daughter of a hero."

She turned her face toward the west. Arthur followed her gaze. Beyond the mountains, past the broad, swampy river valleys, the low rolling hills, the mighty ocean roared. Somewhere hundreds of miles west and south, Lars Nansen faced wind and wave, waiting for his beloved daughter to rejoin him.

Arthur looked back at the girl he loved. He saw what it cost her, the renunciation of everything she held dear. Nay, not everything, for when she turned luminous eyes toward him, dawning radiance replaced pain. She spoke a single word. "Whither."

He caught her to him and bent his head to her upturned face. He heard her soft sigh, felt her lips tremble beneath his own, and felt he had been given a little chunk of heaven. He raised his mouth from hers and she nestled in the shelter of his arms. A silent prayer winged to the skies like a gull caught in an updraft. God grant that *he* might be worthy of her.

That night they told the others of the great love that had found them. Arthur saw understanding in the faces turned toward him. He scanned them, ignoring Jean's fluent chatter about how he knew all along. A slight movement behind him whipped Arthur around to face Strongheart. The Indian held out his hand without speaking. When the evening ended and they headed back to Kayak Jim's, Arthur spoke out of an overflowing heart. "Strongheart, I pray love will one day come to you."

They walked on in the starlight, shadowed by trees whose branches bent low to catch the slightest whisper. For once, the village dogs held their barking tongues. No sound broke the stillness except the slight crunch of Arthur's boots on the needle-forested floor.

Strongheart's moccasins padded silently beside him. When he spoke at last, his voice blended with the mysterious night. "You saved me. You brought me here. Now I am torn. Ivan Romanov has destroyed whole tribes of my people with his whisky and lust. The maiden Naleenah has suffered much because of him. He would have degraded and left her, as he has a hundred others. He and the Indian followers he has enslaved with whisky beat me and left me for dead when I promised to kill him if he ever raised his hand against another Indian maiden." Hatred crept into the small clearing before Kayak's home like a chill wind. Arthur shuddered.

Strongheart went on in the same lifeless voice. "The blood of my ancestors says to grind Romanov beneath my heel as I would a poisonous snake." An unfamiliar note of despair crept into Strongheart's voice. "The love you speak of has already entered my heart. It glows like a comet in the sky. Once Naleenah loved Romanov with all the purity and trust only a good woman possesses. Now her dark eyes show I have found favor with her. She has chosen to follow your God. Sometimes I feel I must seek Him, too, but what about the Russian? The God you worship says not to kill—but a devil threatens this place. Can a man turn his back when evil creeps into the tents of his friends? Is it not better to sacrifice one man than have him destroy many?" Fury raised his voice from its quiet tone.

Arthur desperately searched for words. If ever he had needed wisdom, that time was here in the shadow of a mighty spruce just outside Kayak's door. Starlight spattered between the branches just enough to show the struggle in Strongheart's face. Good versus evil, as old as the world itself. "My friend, I am fighting the same battle as you," Arthur quietly said. "Romanov must be stopped. Yet shedding blood is wrong and—"

A slight scraping sound cut into his words. Strongheart leaped into the open with Arthur just behind. "Who is it?" Strongheart demanded.

"You boys gonna chew the rag all night?" a sleepy voice drawled from the doorway of the log home. Kayak Jim, clad in the red flannel underwear he wore twelve months a year, peered at them. "Y'don't haveta stand outside an' let the dew fall on you."

His appearance ended the conversation but Arthur lay awake for a long time. How much had the old prospector heard? Had the gleam in his eyes been one of knowledge? Arthur tossed restlessly and finally slipped from bed. He huddled by the window and watched the stars go out. In the murky dawn he prayed for help, not just for himself but for the Indian he had come to love as a brother and for those who valiantly worked to bring Christ to Tarnigan.

A rime of white frost formed on the window sill. Hours later, a new day shook itself, yawned, and awakened. The man who kept vigil dreaded it. No one knew what it would bring in this land made perfect by God and sullied by the very men He had created.

fourteen

Early the next morning, so early lights had only begun to show in the windows of Tarnigan, a dark figure detached itself from a building and slunk away on noiseless feet. Like the Grim Reaper in time of plague, the specter slunk from shack to cabin, hut to house. The mysterious figure spared only *Nika Illahee* and Kayak Jim's dwelling place, moving so silently even the village dogs slept on. With the coming of dawn, the wraith disappeared behind a building, undetected except by those it had visited—and one other.

An hour earlier, Inga Nansen had awakened from a nightmare. Sweat drenched her body and soaked her simple white cotton nightgown. Using a trick her father had taught her long ago, Inga inhaled, held her breath, then slowly exhaled. She forced herself to remember the nightmare.

In the dream, she and Arthur again sat on the rock with Indian paintbrush at their feet. He told her of his love and asked her to be his wife. Inga experienced the same emotions in her dream she'd felt when she promised in reality. Only now she didn't look across mountain and plain to the west but down on Tarnigan. A great cloud hung over it, blacker than any she'd seen at sea. It boiled and foamed until she cried out, knowing danger lay in the cloud. Moments later, she and all those she loved battled against a horde of faceless enemies and the words, "Thou shalt not kill" beat into her brain.

Inga's pounding heartbeat gradually slowed to normal

but sleep eluded her. She slid from her bed, wrapped herself in a blanket against the morning chill, and stole to her slightly open second story window. With the shade up to let in the starlight she loved to watch when she retired, it commanded a view of most of Tarnigan. Inga gasped. A shapeless something stole between the buildings. Was it a *man*, crouched into an unnatural position? She strained to see but the shadow remained a dark blob. Not a glimmer or a glance did she get of its face.

Now and then she saw a door open and remain so for a few moments before closing. "It's as if someone is carrying a message," she whispered. The idea caught at her throat. Should she awaken the household? She shook her head. No, for the strange apparition would soon reach *Nika Illahee*.

It did not. After visiting the closest cabin, the man—if it were a man—vanished. Inga waited until daylight came but saw nothing more. Teeth chattering more from excitement than cold, she snuggled back into bed, conscious for the first time of icy toes and fingers.

Inga didn't count on the warm blankets and her troubled night. The next time she opened her eyes, sun and an unaccountable clamor streamed through her window, along with the sound of excited voices. She ran to it and pushed up the sash. Nothing in life had prepared her for what she saw. Half-naked, painted Indians lurched and yipped in the yard below. Roistering, bearded brutes whose faces bore marks of depravity filled the air with obscene jests. Nicolai Anton, Dr. Clifton, and his father stood facing the man Inga instinctively knew to be Ivan Romanov. She gasped. Blond hair and ice-blue eyes shining in the sun, he resembled nothing on earth so much as Lucifer in all his terrible beauty.

A grim-faced Nicolai glanced up at her window.

"Get dressed, Inga."

She saw triumph and something too fearsome to name flame in the Russian's eyes and felt smirched by his look. Slamming down the window and shade, she snatched her closest garments, resenting the time it took to put them on. A quick flick smoothed her tangled braid and she raced downstairs. "What does he want?" she panted.

Pretty Sasha Clifton stood with her arm around Naleenah. "I'm afraid to find out." Dread filled her brown eyes and the Indian girl's dark eyes looked huge in her curiously pale face. A coarse laugh came from outside. The stamping of booted feet followed. The door opened and three men entered, leaving the door open behind them. Dull fury suffused Anton's massive face. Bern scowled like a thundercloud. Benjamin's cheeks had gone paper-white.

"Well?" Sasha's question snapped like a whip wielded by a cruel dog sled owner mushing across frozen ground. "What does he want?"

"He's come for Naleenah. He says he bought her from Tonglaw." Pain and fury twisted Nicolai's face. "The cur! Ivan himself prepared the contract when I paid Tonglaw for Naleenah's freedom more than a year ago. Now he says the contract is invalid because Tonglaw was drunk at the time. Who knows better than he? *Ivan furnished the whiskey.*" Nicolai spread his ham-hands wide. "My people, my people! I thought when we drove Ivan away, they would remain true to the teachings of God. Now Tonglaw and most of the braves are frenzied from drink and ready to kill. Ivan vows they will get no more whisky unless Tonglaw forces me to turn Naleenah over to him. He has given me a half-hour."

Inga felt sick. "You won't let him have her," she cried.

"Of course not!" Nicolai roared. "If only we were not so

few in number! Even Jean and Fanchon have gone trapping."

Benjamin Clifton straightened. Years fell from his shoulders. His colorless eyes gleamed with holy indignation. "We shall overcome." His voice rang in the sudden silence and he took command like a private thrust by necessity into a generalship. "Naleenah is a child of God. She shall be protected to the death, if necessary."

Naleenah freed herself from Sasha and resolutely stepped toward the three men. "I will go with Ivan."

Inga found herself powerless to speak. Like Esther in the Bible, this maiden of the north would sacrifice herself on behalf of those she loved and had made her people.

"Surely you cannot still care for him!" Sasha seized Naleenah and fiercely shook her by the shoulders.

"I despise him." Naleenah aged before their eyes. Her anguished look begged for understanding. "You must not die for me, or shed blood, even that of Ivan Romanov and his beasts." Slim, tragic, she stood before them: a living sacrifice.

Nicolai Anton gave a choked cry. Beads of sweat dotted his forehead. "Naleenah, daughter, it would do no good. Now Romanov wants you. Another time he will demand Little Flower. Bernard, my son, slip out the back way. Bring Strongheart, Arthur, and Kayak Jim. We will hold off the horde as long as we can and then—"

"No need fer that," Kayak drawled from the kitchen doorway. His seamed face split in a grin and he pushed into the room, Strongheart and Arthur at his heels. All three carried rifles. The expression on their faces showed they had heard every word. Strongheart sent Naleenah a look Inga knew she would remember forever. Without a single word, the companion who had sailed on the *Flower of Alaska* and led the expedition to Tarnigan became the Indian girl's protector. While breath remained within him, never would Ivan take her.

"Ho, the house!" Romanov's call interrupted them. "Anton, what is your answer?"

"Stall 'em," Kayak hissed. His eyes gleamed. "Tell him anything, but stall 'em!" He bent forward, clawlike hands twitching.

"You!" Inga's accusation died in her throat, along with all hope. She tried to cry out, to warn the others a traitor stood in their midst. The dark figure she had seen scuttling from house to house now crouched before them. Kayak must have known the very hour Ivan and his followers planned to attack and warned those in the village to remain behind barred doors and not interfere. How could he stand there pretending to be concerned over Naleenah and the others? How could he betray Bern Clifton, who once saved his life? *God, help us all*, she silently prayed.

"Anton, either you come out or we come in." Ivan's taunt floated through the partly open door.

"Stall, I tell ye!" Kayak barked. Rifle ready, he sauntered toward the door. His action caught the others so by surprise, they froze in place. A menacing stillness fell over the outlaws and drunken Indians. Then a new sound encroached on the unnatural stillness, the sound of tramping feet coming at a dead run.

For a moment Inga wondered if God had sent a legion of angels to protect them. The next instant she caught sight of half a hundred armed marchers heading straight toward *Nika Illahee,* rifles and pistols at the ready—each one pointed straight at Ivan Romanov's heart! Understanding burst within her. Kayak Jim was no traitor, but an Alaskan Paul Revere.

He had crept through the dawn and mustered every man and boy old enough to carry a gun to aid their beloved White Father.

The element of surprise served them well. Intimidated by the sight of so many men with weapons, all the Indians except Tonglaw fled from the oncoming threat, falling over one another in their haste to be gone.

Nicolai and Arthur, Benjamin, Strongheart, and Bern followed Kayak outside. The women rushed to the windows. "Say, there, Russian, what'll ye give fer yer life?" Kayak demanded. He grinned in pure devilment.

Romanov's face went dirty white. He instinctively turned toward Nicolai Anton, the man he had betrayed and wronged. He fell to his knees. "For the love of God, don't let them kill me!"

A murmur of contempt ran through the rank gathered from the dregs of society. Inga clutched the edge of a curtain, horrified at the scene but unable to turn her gaze away.

"Once before you promised never to return." Nicolai's voice rolled out like God's judgment on Sodom and Gomorrah. He crossed his arms over his great chest and stood with his feet apart. Benjamin Clifton stood at his right hand; Bern on his left. Arthur and Strongheart flanked Kayak Jim, faces gleaming.

The wild blood of her Norse ancestors beat in Inga's brain. Ivan deserved death and yet—

"Let him go." Naleenah crowded past the men and faced the man who coveted her, until she stood between Romanov and his jury. "I will not have his blood on your hands." She spoke to all, yet Inga knew she directed her words to Strongheart. Mutiny such as she'd never seen in his still face rose, but Naleenah slowly said, "Send him away. He will not dare return." She scornfully waved toward his men.

"Even they spurn Ivan. News will travel on the night wind of Ivan's craven pleading for his life. He is marked forever. Every hand will be against him. One day he will lie in an unmarked coward's grave. Living or dead, from this day Ivan Romanov no longer ceases to exist. I am free." A radiant smile lent beauty beyond description when she turned her head toward Strongheart.

Inga knew Naleenah had just issued Ivan's death sentence. She felt tears not from sympathy, but from knowing the awful punishment the conscienceless man faced from God, if not from his fellowmen.

Nicolai opened his arms. Naleenah flew to them like a small, tired bird after a long flight. "My daughter has spoken well," he announced. "Go, Romanov."

Ivan stumbled to his feet, gaze darting from one to the other. Tonglaw, roused from his stupor by the cowed figure who stumbled toward him, planted himself in the Russian's path. "Whisky."

"You'll get no whisky from me." Romanov sneered with all the arrogance of master to slave. "Get out of my way, you filthy Indian!" He added a round of curses that made Inga cover her ears. Her hands could not shut out Tonglaw's guttural voice. Her fascinated gaze could not leave the Indian's working face. Didn't Ivan realize what a deadly foe he had created? She involuntarily took a step toward the door. Sasha's strong hand held her back.

"Russian give Tonglaw whisky. Now."

A suggestion of foam rimmed Romanov's mouth. "I said no!" He raised a booted foot, sent the Indian sprawling, and turned to send a last vindictive look back toward *Nika Illahee.*

Tonglaw bounded to his feet. His sinewy brown arm clawed at his belt. A slim, keen knife flashed silver in the sunlight, straight toward Ivan's back. The Russian dropped without a sound. Tonglaw snatched his bloodstained knife free and leaped toward Nicolai and the others. "You take Naleenah." Insane from whisky, he raised his arm to throw again.

Kayak fired. With a sickening thud, the bullet slammed into Tonglaw's shoulder, too late to stop the deadly knife. It did change its course. Instead of killing Nicolai, the steel blade plunged deep into Benjamin Clifton's breast.

"Get out of here," one of Romanov's men screeched.

Inga barely heard him. She pelted out the door, Sasha just behind her. Bern had already dropped to his father's side. Trembling hands tore away Benjamin's bloody shirt. Sickness washed over his face and he groaned.

Praying for control, Inga knelt beside him. "Did the knife nick the heart?" She pressed both hands over the wound to slow the spurting blood.

"I don't know. I'll have to go in. God in heaven, how can I operate on my own father?" His cry sounded loud in the stillness.

Before the echoes died, Arthur leaped to his side. "I'm a surgeon. I'll do it."

Hope flared in Bern's dark eyes, then turned to ashes. "Only a man skilled in the most delicate surgery can perform this operation. Heart surgery is too new a skill. . .only a doctor who had the best training, the most skill and daring. . ." He looked at his shaking hands. "I know of only one man beside myself who could do it. Even then, it might avail nothing."

Arthur had never dreamed the revelation of his identity

would come like this. He gripped Bern's arm. "Bern, that man is here. *I am Arthur Baldwin.*"

"*You?*" Bern's dark face blanched. "Then that's why I— how—?"

A power not his own entered Arthur's soul. "There's no time for explanations. Pull yourself together, man. I'll need you to assist. Strongheart has some training, Inga more. With the help of God we are going to save your father's life!"

Nicolai, Naleenah, Sasha, and Kayak Jim silently followed Arthur's barked orders. The dining room table became a surgical table. After thoroughly scrubbing, Arthur and his two assistants plus Bern stood beside their patient. Nicolai Anton's rich voice came from behind them. "God, grant these Thy children the skill to save one who has served Thee for so long."

Despite concentrating on the job ahead, Arthur soon realized once surgery began, Bern Clifton was no longer Benjamin's son but an assistant surgeon. He and Arthur worked as smoothly as two pair of hands directed by the same mind—in this case, the same guiding Spirit. At one point, Arthur despaired. Could they repair the damage before Benjamin bled to death? They must. He hadn't traveled all these thousands of miles to fail his friend in an hour of need that by comparison made the Philadelphia incident the prank of a naughty child. Even when Clifton's pulse faltered, he continued.

"I can close," Bern said. The eyes above his gauze surgical mask showed firmness. Arthur silently stepped aside, feeling drained. He watched Bern set sutures with steady hands and at last strip away his gloves and remove his mask. Only then did he let slip the discipline imposed by long years of study, practice, and the refusal to give up while life lasted. Bern's voice shook when he said, "He's in God's hands."

Nika Illahee became the stage for a second battle. Arthur and Bern fought for the life of the man who had been father to both. Days and nights blurred. Benjamin's temperature soared, fell, and rose again. Babblings showed how much he had suffered far more clearly than Clifton would ever have done. At last his fever dwindled. He still tossed and muttered but now his undying belief in forgiveness through Jesus Christ overcame all else.

During the crisis time, Inga hadn't been able to persuade either doctor to rest and allow her to care for the patient. Once he grew better, she drove them away. "Strongheart and I will care for him," she promised. "If there is any sign of a problem, we'll send for one or both of you."

Arthur sheepishly grinned at Bern, yawned, and headed for Kayak Jim's and the room he hadn't occupied since the tragedy. He'd dozed in a chair just enough to keep going. Exhaustion deeper than anything he'd ever known took him past gossiping villagers who called out the news that Tonglaw resided in a strong, barred building, waiting for the long arm of the law to reach Tarnigan. He barely managed a nod to a disgruntled Jean and Fanchon Langlois, even when the French-Canadian grumbled, "The fight of a lifetime and where was Jean Langlois? Out catching the little animals of the woods!" He waved to Strongheart, who walked proudly beside Naleenah, yawned, and kept going.

Twenty-four hours later, Arthur awakened to find Bern sitting at the foot of his bed, watching him with inscrutable eyes. Not a trace of a smile brightened his craggy face.

Quick alarm spread through Arthur. "Your father?"

"No. Me."

All the newly found hope of being forgiven that Arthur had felt building during the time they worked as brothers now fled. He swung his feet over the side of the bed and stared at the man he loved more now than he ever had in all their days together.

"I can never repay you," Bern said in a monotone.

Arthur crashed headfirst into the other's reserve. "I don't want your gratitude. I want your forgiveness."

Bern looked shocked. "You've had it for a long time." His black eyes softened into tenderness.

"Because I was here when your father needed my surgical skills." Grief welled within Arthur. He thought he'd reached the depths of pain and remorse during his years of searching. Now he realized the cup he drank from surpassed anything he'd ever known. He longed to throw it aside. He could not. He must hold it to his lips and taste the final, bitter dregs. So great was his agony, he barely heard Bern speak.

"I forgave you months ago," Bern brokenly said. "All that back there in Philadelphia is from a different lifetime." He rose, face humble. "God gave us a precious friendship. I transgressed over the desire for fame and a woman not worthy to be called by that name. You retaliated. We became enemies. Now God has brought us together by strange paths. Arthur, I shudder to think where we would be if none of it had happened. I'd never have known Sasha, or this wild, unforgettable land, or God as I do now." He hesitated. "If you could go back to the way we were, would you?"

The poignant question rang in Arthur's heart. Oh, to start afresh! To wipe out the long years as a wandering Judas and return to his happy boyhood when he dedicated himself toward bringing peace and joy into a dark, sin-bound world. But what would life be without Inga? Without Jean and his

Fanchon, Captain Nansen, Strongheart? Could he return to his careless days of dallying with trifles while the Savior who died for him sadly stood watching from the shadows?

Arthur shook his head. "Would you?" He felt as if the earth stopped rotating on its axis to wait for Bern's answer.

The reply came without a second's hesitation, like the sharp, clean cut of a shining scalpel. "Never."

Strong hands met, clasped, parted, signifying brotherhood tried in the crucible of despair, purified by the cleansing fire of God. Arthur's long search had ended.

epilogue

Rising wind molded Inga Nansen Baldwin's dress to her rigidly held body. It flirted with the sunny plaits wrapped around her shapely head and restored sparkle to eyes blue as a Norwegian fjord. "Hero's daughter," by name and upbringing, Inga stood on the dock at Vancouver, one hand raised, heart torn between love for husband and father. Arthur had kept his promise and taken her back to Lars and the *Flower of Alaska*. Lars married them at sea and all through autumn and winter they had sailed with him. They gloried in sunrises and sunsets, riding the storms with the same high courage they employed to meet whatever life storms lay ahead.

From his position at the helm, Lars watched Inga and Arthur dwindle to doll size. He had asked them not to watch the ship out of sight. He saw them turn to face northwest. Far beyond civilization, Strongheart and Naleenah, Bern and Sasha, Jean, Fanchon, and their new son Noble Langlois, Benjamin Clifton, Kayak Jim, and the great-hearted Nicolai Anton waited.

Lars's keen gaze riveted on his daughter's still figure. Only the set of her shoulders, rigid and square as a soldier at attention, kept him from going back. Dreams stirred within him and he smiled. Before the hand of life fell too heavily on his shoulder, he would visit Tarnigan. One day, sure-footed grandchildren would walk the deck of the *Flower of Alaska*, as Astrid and Inga had done. God willing, he'd live to see it. Setting his course by the westering sun, Lars steamed out of the harbor into open water.

Arthur tenderly kissed his wife and took her hand. "Come." They turned their faces toward the North Star and faced the bright open sea of their lives together.

A Letter To Our Readers

Dear Reader:

In order that we might better contribute to your reading enjoyment, we would appreciate your taking a few minutes to respond to the following questions. When completed, please return to the following:

Rebecca Germany, Managing Editor
Heartsong Presents
P.O. Box 719
Uhrichsville, Ohio 44683

1. Did you enjoy reading *Flower of Alaska*?
   ❑ Very much. I would like to see more books by this author!
   ❑ Moderately
      I would have enjoyed it more if _____
      _____

2. Are you a member of **Heartsong Presents**? ❑Yes ❑No
   If no, where did you purchase this book?_____
   _____

3. What influenced your decision to purchase this book? (Check those that apply.)

   ❑ Cover   ❑ Back cover copy

   ❑ Title   ❑ Friends

   ❑ Publicity   ❑ Other_____

4. How would you rate, on a scale from 1 (poor) to 5 (superior), the cover design?_____

5. On a scale from 1 (poor) to 10 (superior), please rate the following elements.

    __Heroine   __Plot

    __Hero   __Inspirational theme

    __Setting   __Secondary characters

6. What settings would you like to see covered in **Heartsong Presents** books?_____

_____

_____

7. What are some inspirational themes you would like to see treated in future books?_____

_____

_____

8. Would you be interested in reading other **Heartsong Presents** titles? ❑ Yes ❑ No

9. Please check your age range:
❑ Under 18 ❑ 18-24 ❑ 25-34
❑ 35-45 ❑ 46-55 ❑ Over 55

10. How many hours per week do you read? _____

Name _____

Occupation_____

Address_____

City_____ State_____ Zip _____

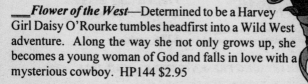

Colleen L. Reece

The Flower Chronicles

___*Flower of the West*—Determined to be a Harvey Girl Daisy O'Rourke tumbles headfirst into a Wild West adventure. Along the way she not only grows up, she becomes a young woman of God and falls in love with a mysterious cowboy. HP144 $2.95

___*Flower of the North*—Pursuing a call to doctor in the harsh and and unforgiving Northwest, Bernard Clifton must begin to discover what he is really made of, and what is most important in life. Will a true and worthy love at last claim Bernard's anguished heart? HP159 $2.95

___*Flower of Alaska*—Inga Nansen has waited many long years to rejoin her father on his seagoing ship, cruising the picturesque ports of the great Northwest. But now her heart is being pulled in a different direction. The love of her life is bound for the harsh and unforgiving Alaska wilderness. HP187 $2.95

......Hearts♥ng ......

HEARTSONG PRESENTS TITLES AVAILABLE NOW:

(If ordering from this page, please remember to include it with the order form.)

··········Presents ········